IS IT WORTH ANYTHING?

ROSTERS LTD, LONDON

IS IT WORTH ANYTHING?

Stephen Ellis

ROSTERS LTD, LONDON

Published by Rosters Ltd
60 Welbeck St
London, W1

First edition 1989
© Rosters Ltd

ISBN 0 948032 56 1

Filmset by Gwynne Printers, Hurstpierpoint, West Sussex
Printed and bound in Great Britain by Cox & Wyman Ltd, Reading

Cover credits: 'Beanos', the Record Dealers; Pollocks Toy Museum
and J. Wedgewood.

Contents

Acknowledgements

For all her help and guidance my sincere thanks go to Victoria Wolcough of Christie's. Without her this book would not have been possible. Thank goodness she had the vision to see what some of her competitors could not. Pictures and help with the words were also supplied by many of the people working for Christie's whose assistance I gratefully acknowledge. Many other sources are mentioned in the specialist chapters and are too numerous to list but their support has also been much appreciated. A special mention must be made for David Lashmar of Beanos, though, since his knowledge on records gave me the encouragement I needed in the first place. Other pictures have been provided by Memories of Hendon, the London office of IPM Promotions, by Seaby's, by Sotheby's and the Topham Picture Library (chapter eight). Finally, a word for the publisher and her staff. It is amazing how they have suffered on my behalf and I only trust that they feel, as I do, it has all been worthwhile.

Introduction

Every home has one: an attic, a back cupboard or just a drawer where keep-sakes are tucked away. Those things that remind us of times gone by. For many parents that little store – or not so little in some cases – holds memories of their children and the different stages they went through as they grew up.

Toys, stamp collections, postcards, old records and the like are simply left to gather dust. It is not until people are moving home that these treasures are unearthed and in many cases they do not see the light of day until the 'hoarder' has passed on and relatives discover the hidden treasures. That's when papers like the *Mirror* are sent letters with the plaintive plea: 'Is it worth anything?' Sad to say in these modern times few newspapers or magazines have the staff or facilities to answer individual letters but I'm pleased to say that does not stop people from writing. In my position on the *Mirror* I use the odd spare moment to read as many of these letters as possible. Many of the best ideas for articles come from this source. So, too did this book. For it reflects those many letters about the hidden hoards turned up when houses are cleared for one reason or another.

All too frequently, of course, what we regard as valuable because of its sentimental attachments is of little monetary worth. However, sometimes there are diamonds in the coalmine, for example people who've discovered long lost paintings by famous artists. Such cases are rare. What most of us are more likely to find are items that, while not worth a king's ransom, could well reward a little time and effort spent investigating their value.

I hope that many of those who read the following pages have the good fortune to find the odd treasure amongst their hidden keepsakes. Those that don't I feel sure will still enjoy browsing through the pages recalling their own childhoods and wondering: 'What if I'd kept those old postcards or cigarette cards?' Too late now to rue the eagerness that threw out those unwanted toys or that gave in to fashion and was happy to see the back of those old medals. However, maybe a look at what has passed you by will make you pause before you next come to throw out all that 'old junk'. For hidden away you may have a postcard, coin or Toby jug which collectors would give their back teeth – or, more to the point, a fair amount of cash – to own!

Before you delve into the pages, however, a few words of warning about valuing your finds. In researching this book I contacted most of the large auction houses and some of the specialist dealers. Despite their claims to be 'only too happy' to help by valuing items for the public free of charge I found they were not so keen when it really came down to it. The giant exception was Christie's whose staff have been invaluable in helping to write this book and I would like to take time out now to thank all those whose patience I must have tried over and over again when I simply could not grasp some of the, to them, simple aspects of their specialisms. I also recommend readers to contact Christie's should they have items they wish to be valued.

Now to prices. Throughout the book I have referred to values that match what it is thought a collector would pay for the items in question. By reading the specialist magazines you may be able to contact a collector directly and then the prices quoted will be close to those offered. Similarly if you find something which is put up for auction, and there are people on the day who are interested in your find, then you should get the amounts I've indicated and sometimes even more. There will, of course, be a commission to pay to the auctioneers, though. Should you decide to go to a dealer with your discovery then you cannot expect him to pay the same price. He will want to allow for his profit margin and may need to keep the item for some time before he finds a buyer. For this reason you should not expect more than a half the figures quoted and two-thirds would be the very highest in normal circumstances.

It is silly to send most items you might unearth through the post. If they are of value you will be heartbroken should they go astray. In many cases a photograph plus a full description will be sufficient for the experts to give you some guide to the value, though you will ultimately need to take the item itself along to get a specific price. When you send off details and want a reply you should enclose a stamped, addressed envelope. What you must remember is that condition is vital in most cases so the expert's valuation may not be accurate if you fail to tell him about a major crack or some other damage. The only person you will be fooling, of course, is yourself.

As in all cases where money is concerned other people will be all too eager to make a profit out of you. Never sell to the first person who comes along and certainly avoid 'knockers' – the people who come to the door and offer you cash on the spot. You can be sure that if they are interested in getting their hands on it then so will other people. Also, don't be fooled when they say "It's not really worth anything but if you throw it in with the other bits and pieces I'll give you an extra fiver." While I have tried to highlight some of the finds you might make which could be worth selling there are also many where there is no great value other than a sentimental one. If this is the case, do not be deterred. Even these may end up as collectors' items in the years to come and then they will justify the space they have taken up in the years between.

Finally my thanks to all the *Mirror* readers who continue to send us such interesting letters. They are the spark that started this idea and, hopefully I will be able to write a further volume to include some other subjects on which they want information.

CHAPTER ONE:
CHINA

Blue and White Pottery

Staffordshire blue and white tureen cover with lion finial, circa 1820
Source: Christie's, South Kensington.

According to the people who travel the country valuing 'finds' for the big auction houses and for the television programme The Antiques Roadshow, one of the most popular items they come across is blue and white pottery. It seems everyone has some tucked away somewhere, much of it with the famous 'Willow' pattern. Unfortunately, the mere fact that there is so much around shows that it is unlikely to be of great value. However, the exceptions are pieces that date from before the middle of the nineteenth century. For the inexperienced eye it is quite difficult to judge with any accuracy the exact age of pottery so this is an area where it is vital to get expert help. As well as auction houses like Christie's, we have listed a couple of other sources for information on the subject at the end of this section.

In this day and age of mass production when putting a pattern on a plate is commonplace and relatively simple it is difficult to imagine the problems facing early potters, who, inspired by the fine hand painted ceramics imported from China, wanted to produce attractively printed wares. It was in the late eighteenth century that the method for transferring prints to porcelain and pottery was first developed. The process involved engraving a design on a flat copper plate, transferring the design to strong tissue paper using a warm oily ink, pressing this against the ceramic surface and then putting the whole thing in cold water. That helped to set the ink and allowed the paper to be removed easily. At first such transfers were only carried out on already glazed surfaces. However, this meant that it was far from permanent and so it was only really acceptable for display items since constant use or simply frequent washing would damage the print. Ways to overcome this problem were examined in virtually every large factory and it is not clear who came up with the eventual solution, but it was one adopted throughout the five Staffordshire towns where blue and white printed ware has been produced from the early 1800s to the present day.

At this time the pottery was akin to Ford's later cars in that you could have any colour printing so long as it was blue. One of the reasons was the ready availability of cobalt, but blue was also very popular following on from the Chinese tradition and it was one of the colours that could withstand the heat of the furnaces. Once the copper plates had been inked and the design transferred to the tissue paper, this was transferred to the unglazed pottery. An initial heating fixed the ink, then it was glazed and fired again. Very early examples may well appear over inked or blurred because there was no way of controlling the amount of ink either held in the engraving or transferred to the tissue. Once the principle had been established the potter's next task was to find the right designs. Most of the early examples were based on Chinese patterns and Thomas Minton, one of the foremost designers at the time, is credited with developing the famous Willow pattern. This is still used today and shows a pagoda with pavilion or tea house on the right in front of an apple tree. In the centre a willow tree leans over a three-arched bridge on which three figures are crossing. In the top left a covered boat crewed by one man floats in front of a small island, and there are two doves in the sky. In the foreground there is a zig-zag fence.

In the Dictionary Of Blue and White Printed Pottery by A. W. Coysh and R. K. Henrywood, the following explanation of the pottery is put forward:

'A Chinese mandarin Li-Chi lived in a pagoda beneath an apple tree. He had a beautiful daughter Koong-Shee, who was to marry an elderly merchant named Ta Jin. However, she fell in love with her father's secretary, Chang, who was dismissed when it was discovered that they had been having clandestine meetings. Koong-Shee and Chang then eloped and, helped by the Mandarin's gardener, they are seen crossing the bridge which spans the river. The boat is used to approach Chang's house but the furious mandarin discovers their retreat. They are pursued and about to be beaten to death

13

when the Gods take pity on them, and turn them into a pair of doves.'

Fanciful, maybe, but just the sort of thing to appeal to the Victorians who filled their homes with examples of willow pattern ware which was made by a host of potteries throughout the nineteenth and twentieth centuries. Soon the designers turned to other subjects for inspiration starting with flowers and views of foreign places and then, closer to home, British scenes, many based on paintings by famous artists of the time. The number of potteries producing the ware had also greatly increased with Welsh, Yorkshire, Scottish and Tyne and Wear works joining in.

Staffordshire blue and white tureen, circa 1820.
Source: Christie's, South Kensington.

Even so the price of the pottery ensured that it was a middle class item but there was a limit to this market. So cheaper versions were introduced and patterns became more standardised – hence the huge amounts of Willow that still exist. Some say this was the start of the decline in the style of pottery – around 1840 – when colours other than blue were also introduced. A final blow came in 1842 when the Copyright Act was passed. Many of the designs previously had been based on pictures or copied from one pottery to the next. All this became illegal. So the makers invented their own designs all based on a simple formula. You had to have water, a building and a tree, usually with hills or mountains in the background and people in the foreground. In essence a simplified Willow pattern. By the turn of the century all that was left of the style were the basic designs as potteries turned to new styles.

However, today's trends for a return to more rustic looks has created a great deal of interest in early blue and white pottery so you can expect to get a fair price. Surprisingly perhaps, condition is not everything, at least as far as the rare early nineteenth century patterns are concerned. In these cases even repaired items can fetch several pounds so don't automatically write off your discovery. Dinner plates on average will fetch around £30 and you may get as much as £100 for dishes. However, that's just a rough guide since individual items may be of specific interest because of the pottery at which they were made or the particular design. Sporting prints usually fetch higher prices. A Copeland and Garrett oblong meat-dish with Shooting a Leopard went for £440 in a recent Christie's auction. A rare Enoch Wood & Sons oval meat dish with Hunting Polar Bears dating from around 1825 fetched £385 at auction in 1987. As the glaze was lifting it was described as 'crazed' meaning it was covered in a network of thin lines. A pierced basket with the same print went for £352 in the same sale even though it has been restored.

Named views of houses or places are also in demand

so are likely to be priced higher. So too are unusually shaped pieces like footbaths, flasks or feeding cups which sell for upwards of £30. An oval two-handled footbath with an elephant pattern dating from 1825 brought £825 when it was sold at auction a couple of years ago. Part of the design looked to be damaged showing an odd half flower. However, Christie's experts point out that this happened when a pattern was adapted from a print designed for a flat meat dish so that it could be put on a rounded surface. It does not detract from the value. The place of manufacture is important with Spode examples fetching high prices because of their consistently high quality. However, do not assume that the same design was always produced by the same potter. The difference in the potter can be reflected in the price. As for the inevitable Willow pattern, or similar Oriental scenes, only the very early nineteenth century pieces are of interest and even these are only worth a few pounds. You might be lucky enough to get £40 for a meat dish but that would be unusual. When it comes to the most recent finds, sad to say they are fairly unsaleable.

Goss China

William Henry Goss and his eldest son Adolphus spawned a whole industry when they produced the first porcelain holiday souvenirs featuring coats of arms. Their original designs were a far cry from today's cheap and cheerful keepsakes and can fetch quite high prices at auction. Goss china was a great collector's item in Edwardian times so there is a good chance you'll come across some in the attic of an old house or, indeed, on the mantlepiece in granny's front room.

When William Goss decided to set up his own pottery works in 1858 he was entering a highly competitive market. The area around Stoke, the

From left: A Goss parian bust of W. H. Goss, £100-£120; an early Goss parian figure of a shepherd boy, £300-£500; a Goss parian bust of General Gordon £120-£160.
Source: Christie's, South Kensington.

Potteries as it was known, was awash with firms – as many as 120 say some experts – trying to make a living out of china. In fact William had gained much of his knowledge working as chief artist and designer at rival potters Copeland. So the trick was to come up with something different. One of William's answers was to sell his own formula coloured enamels to other potteries. He also devised new recipes for the glazing and the gilding as well as other aspects of his china, making it unique and in a different class to that produced by his rivals. Throughout the years these secrets were closely guarded though there was one breech when eleven Goss workers were lured to the Belleek firm in Ireland's County Fermanagh in 1863. To this day china from that factory is very similar to the Goss products.

There is no doubting that William was successful but he was also a little set in his ways. So when young Adolphus first came up with the idea of souvenirs his father's response was less than enthusiastic. However, Adolphus could see the potential. More and more people were travelling to different parts of the country thanks to new laws forcing employers to give workers holidays, the availability of cheap railway travel and the love of the seaside displayed by Queen Victoria and the Prince Regent. He came up with the idea of making the souvenirs shaped like pieces found in local museums and bearing the local coat of arms. They were to be sold by one appointed 'agent' at just one shop in each area. His father, who was a typical stern Victorian, did not believe that the scheme would work. However, he was eventually persuaded to give Adolphus a chance to test the market after seeing some prototypes.

William was proved wrong and the public responded immediately to the idea of souvenirs with coats of arms on them, and within no time at all demand for the heraldic ware was outstripping that for the original parian figures and busts. Indeed, so great was the demand that the factory had to be completely rebuilt between 1881 and 1886 trebling the floor space. Eventually the range was extended to allow the agents to sell all the different shaped items, though still only with their local coats of arms on them. It is worth noting that models bearing the marching coats of arms appropriate to the named model are now highly prized and will fetch as much as 50 per cent more than an unmatched model.

Adolphus was also responsible for the introduction of the Goss cottages, the first three – Ann Hathaway's, Shakespeare's Birthplace and Burns's Ayrshire Cottage – being introduced in 1893. A Shakespeare's House model will fetch between £70 and £160 today depending on the particular style. However, Adolphus was spending more and more of his time organising the outlets to sell Goss items, acting as a company rep and salesman which he believed was vital. He fell out with his father when he began to call himself 'Goss Boss'.

There was also a family feud between William and the next eldest son Godfrey, and so when he died in 1906 William left the factory to the third son Victor. Unfortunately Victor died in a riding accident seven years later and it was the youngest son, Huntley, who was left to steer the firm through the First World War and the great depression. He introduced a number of special Great War items, including a tank and bombs to try, in an attempt to stave off the inevitable. Sad to say in 1929 Huntley sold the firm and the rights to its trademark to rivals Cauldon Potteries. His father had always been acknowledged as a good employer and had fought for better working conditions and the elimination of child labour. Huntley kept up the traditions, using some of the cash to pay off all the bills and see that workers' salaries were up to date.

A new boss, Harold Taylor Robinson, took over in 1931 but was already feeling the strain of being the area's largest potter. He was declared bankrupt in 1932 and the firm went into receivership in 1934. Other potteries stepped in to fill the breech making a range of items under the Goss mark, though it was never quite the same. During this time a number of commemorative mugs and beakers, including some Toby jugs worth up to £130 today, were produced. In addition there was a popular range of cottage pottery. Prices for individual cottage pottery items range from less than £20 to £75 or so for some posy holders. There were also some figures and animals produced including coloured crinoline flower girls in the Doulton style which are now worth between £100 and £300 each. The factory finally closed as a pottery in 1939 but the Goss ovens are still there, the subject of a conservation order.

Early Goss pieces have just the name W H Goss printed on the bottom. In 1862 the printed goshawk emblem was introduced and remained on pieces

Left: A Goss model of the Goss ovan, Stoke-on-Trent, £120-£150. Right: A Goss model of St Catherine's Chapel, Abbotsbury, £300-£400.
Source: Christie's, South Kensington.

through to the end of then era. It was the large winged bird that gave rise to the local name of the potteries, the Falcon works. For just one year, 1967, William Goss tied up with a Mr Peake and items were stamped with both names. Condition is of paramount importance when it comes to Goss china. Worn gilding, fading, chips, cracks and firing flaws will result in much lower prices when you try to sell them. The attractive cottages, for instance, are often found with a chimney missing which can knock as much as three-quarters off the value. Hairline cracks are also often in evidence on pieces. Such damage can halve the value of your find.

Renovation is possible and this will increase the amount it will fetch. However, experts will still not pay as much as they would for an undamaged original. Do take a close and critical look at any find you make. There is a vast difference between fading and oxidisation. the former happens when the item is exposed to sunlight and there is nothing that can be done to reverse the process. However, if you find Goss china hidden in an attic or an old trunk it may well have been wrapped in newspaper or kept well out of the daylight. When you uncover it the oxygen in the air will react with it and can cause a brown film to form. This can be removed using detergent but you must be very gentle. Make sure you thoroughly rinse it after cleaning.

There are effectively three periods of Goss china: 1858 to 1887, 1881 to 1934 and 1930 to 1939. The first covers the time when William owned and ran the factory. Early products included terracotta ware, jewelled items, famous portrait busts – many made of parian, a fine white procelain – and Victorian unglazed figurines. A Prince of Wales bust dated 1875 could fetch up to £2,000 today. Some items have a floral decoration added to them and this would generally raise the price by £50 to £75. A terracotta bust of Robert Burns is reckoned to be worth around £400. The items with coats of arms on them were first introduced towards the end of the first period but the bulk of this ware was produced in the second period.

The second period covers the years when William's sons were in charge. This was the most prolific time and saw the explosion in the production of heraldic ware – including historic models and special shapes – leading to what the experts call 'mass production', though it was a far cry in those days from how we would interpret the phrase now. This period also takes in dolls, miniatures, cottages, crosses, fonts and animals. Pieces from this period range widely in value. You'll be lucky to get more than £20 for one of the smaller Bath Roman Ewers or a Bournemouth Fine Cone. However, a Chester Roman Urn might fetch £300 and you could get £700 or more for a Chester Roman Vase.

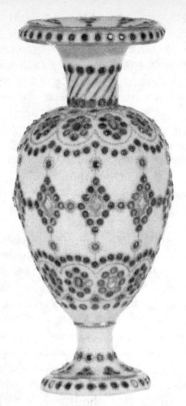

Rare early Goss jewelled vase, £500-£700.
Source: Christie's, South Kensington.

When Harold Taylor Robinson took over the firm
he set about trying to revitalise flagging sales by
introducing heavier and more colourful ranges of
pottery. He also allowed other factories to make items
under the Goss mark. So the third period takes in
their, in some cases, poor imitations of the originals.
As acknowledged expert Nicholas Pine puts it:
'Although the coats of arms still continued to appear
on a range of vases, utility shapes, comical animals and

buildings, they are very different from those of the previous period and values are generally lower.' Items like bowls and ashtrays were included in the range during this period and some pieces are worth no more than £10. However, a Scottish Lion on a square ashtray base, for instance, should be worth around £100.

It is important to realise that the success of the Goss heraldic wares led to a host of copies from other potteries both in this country and in Germany. Many are easily identifiable since they do not have the same attention to detail and are not of the same quality nor do they have as good a finish. However, some unscrupulous people in recent years, following the growing interest in Goss china, have turned these imitations into Goss fakes with the addition of the familiar trademark. If your find has been hidden away in a cupboard or attic it is unlikely to have been treated in this way.

Finally, it is worth laying to rest one of the great misnomers connected to Goss. The popular term used to describe the famous heraldic ware is 'crested china'. However, a crest is just part of a coat of arms whereas most Goss pieces are decorated by complete coats of arms so, in truth, they should be called 'armorial'. That said, most people will know what you're talking about if you speak of crested china.

Contacts

Goss has become so collectable that the big auction houses like Christie's regularly hold sales including this attractive china and there are also many dealers specialising in Goss ware. The Goss Collectors Club publishes a regular monthly magazine, holds regional meetings and postal auctions. Details from Ken Taylor, Editor and Registrar, 'La Pipeterie', 12 Harts

Gardens, Guildford, Surrey GU2 6QA. Telephone: 0483 504173.

Goss & Crested China are dealers in heraldic china. They are open normal working hours but suggest you should telephone to make an appointment if you are travelling any distance or want personal attention. Lynda and Nicholas Pine run the business and also publish Goss & Crested China, a monthly illustrated sales catalogue which is available on subscription. Their address is 62 Murray Road, Horndean, Hampshire PO87 9JL. Telephone: Horndean (0705) 597440.

The duo also run Milestone Publications which publishes a number of books on the subject. Much of the information contained in this chapter has been gleaned from Nicholas Pine's Concise Encyclopaedia and Price Guide to Goss China.

Other dealers include Midland Goss (Betty Malin), Warwick Antiques Centre, 22 High Street, Warwick, 0926 495704 and Goss China (Yorkshire), The Station House, Driffield, East Yorks, 0377 47042.

Japanese Eggshell Porcelain Tea Sets

This heading will, no doubt, have attracted a number of readers who immediately rushed off to look at that fantastic tea set a relative brought home when travelling in the orient or when there on military service. Even those toughened by years of examining people's priceless treasures – only to have to break the news that they are pleasant but unlikely to attract attention from a buyer – are startled by the numbers of these sets that are brought to them for valuation when they tour around the country.

The title 'eggshell' gives away much of the secret. They are made of the very thinnest porcelain and so are no good for holding the heat. They are also highly fragile and, whilst they look attractive, are not of any real value. According to the experts at Christie's few people accept such a verdict and flaunt off convinced that someone is out to cheat them. There is little that can be said or written to appease such people who have clearly treasured their 'present from the East' for many years. By all means display these tea sets for they are decorative, but if they are damaged do not shed tears. Please don't bother to contact anyone in the hope that they will have a different view. While there are some very fine examples of Japanese ceramics these tea sets are not valuable heirlooms – at least not at the moment.

Toby Jugs

Two late 18th century Staffordshire Toby Jugs.
Estimate £400-£600.
Source: Christie's, South Kensington.

If you need a cautionary tale about what can happen when you go rummaging through old attics then look no further than Tom Power, a property developer from Muswell Hill. Fourteen years ago he discovered three toby jugs in his attic and today he has one of the finest collections of Royal Doulton character jugs in the country boasting some 400 worth several thousand pounds. Although it is clear that character jugs developed from the cream-coloured saltglaze stoneware figures made in the area known as the Staffordshire Potteries, it is more difficult to trace the origins of the Toby design. It seems most likely to have derived from an engraving of Toby Fillpot (Philpot) who featured in a poem, 'Metamorphosis' by Italian Geronimo Amalteo which was translated in 1761 by Rev. Francis Hawes for his Original Poems and Translations. The translation was sub-titled Toby Reduced and recounted the life and death of a hearty drinker. The last verse reads:

'His body, when long in the Ground it had lain,
And time into Clay had resolv'd it again,
A Potter found out in its Covert so snug
And with part of fat Toby he form'd this brown Jug.'

The Toby design was based on a mezzotint by Robert Dighton and showed a fat Toby with his brimming tankard in one hand and a clay pipe in the other. Other suggestions as to the model for Toby jugs have included Sir Toby Belch in Shakespeare's Twelfth Night and Uncle Toby in Lawrence Sterne's Tristram Shandy. There are also several suggestions as to the real person on whom Toby Fillpot was based. Favourite is Harry Elwes who is reckoned to have drunk 2,000 gallons of beer from a plain silver tankard during his life, eventually dying 'as big as a barrell butt' around the middle of the eighteenth century. Still, another suggestion is Yorkshire farmer Paul Parnell, who is said to have downed £9,000 of liquor during his life.

Not only is there confusion about the model for

Toby jugs but there seems to be considerable doubt in people's minds as to who made the first one. Those most frequently mentioned include John Astbury of Shelton, Thomas Whieldon of Fenton and Ralph Wood of Burslem. In his book British Toby Jugs, acknowledged expert Vic Schuler knocks down the myth that either Astbury or Whieldon were the originators and even casts doubts on whether many of the Toby Jugs attributed to them were, in fact, made by them. He also points out that Ralph Wood spent most of his life working for Wedgwood and doubts whether he ever produced his own Tobies and figures despite the fact many late eighteenth century figures have R Wood and Ra Wood Burslem on them.

Ralph Wood did have two sons, however. One, also named Ralph, who is credited with a lot of old Tobies but, again, Mr Schuler suggests this is unlikely – and he bases most of his arguments on considerable research into the Wood family carried out by Pat Halfpenny. It is the other son, John Wood Snr who is now being put forward as the most likely to have started and perpetuated the Toby Jug craze. There is evidence that he sold some in 1786 but other members of the family including Ralph Wood III and a cousin, Enoch Wood, were all potters and were probably involved in producing Tobies.

Certainly there were many Staffordshire potters involved in making Toby Jugs and there is no evidence to suggest that all the jugs of one style came from a particular pottery. Indeed, the reverse is probably true since skilled modellers often worked for more more than one pottery. Also, the life expectancy of potteries in those days was short and moulds would be sold off to a rival whe one went bankrupt. Nor was Toby production restricted to Staffordshire. The Swansea pottery in Wales, the Portobello near Edinburgh and some in the Yorkshire area all made Tobies.

Unfortunately many of these early Tobies were not marked with the potter's initials so it is difficult to identify them with their maker. However, some old Tobies were marked so if you come across any names like Palmer, Wilson, Neale, Pratt, Davenport or Walton – as well as Wood, of course – they are likely to be of interest to collectors and probably date from the late eighteenth century or beginning of the nineteenth.

There is considerable variation in the size, style and colouring of the jugs and all these factors play an important part in valuing your discovery. The ordinary Toby Jug stands about 9 to 10 inches high and weighs around 2.75 pounds. If it is noticeably lighter then it might well date back to the eighteenth century. The quality and colouring of the glaze can also affect the value. There are also female Tobies which were modelled after Martha Gunn, a very large and famous Brighton bathing lady. That was in the days when you used a bathing machine – a small hut on wheels – which was operated usually by someone of the same sex. However, Martha is reputed to have regularly dipped the Prince of Wales which is said to account for the fact that she has fleur de lis feathers on her hat. To find an original Martha Gunn made by Wood or Walton would be a truly valuable discovery since it is likely to fetch more than £1,000. Other female Tobies include Drunken Sal, the Gin Woman, the Hurdy Gurdy Player, the Female Snuff-Taker and the Lady Toper. The latter was made by W. Kent between 1900 and 1962 and is likely to be worth around £50.

In fact, many different characters have been depicted on Toby Jugs over the years. There is the Prince Hal or King Hal jug which is usually around 15 inches tall and is worth at least £1,250. Other characters include the Thin Man which dates from the eighteenth century and is likely to fetch more than

£2,000, the Postboy which is reckoned to be poorly modelled but quite rare and worth over £100, the Soldier from 1830 which is also likely to sell for more than £100 and the George Whitfield or Nightwatchman. One, the Unfrocked Parson which shows a man sitting with a wine glass in his left hand and a jug in his right is sometimes called the Drunken Parson and is thought to have been inspired by a print by William Hogarth in A Harlot's Progress. A slightly damaged one of these was sold in 1985 for £410. Some real people were honoured in jug form such as Lord Howe naval hero of the 'Glorious First of June', Admiral Vernon – the man who started the idea of navy rum – and John Wesley. However, the most popular figure to be portrayed on Toby Jugs this century was Sir Winston Churchill.

Although most Tobies are seated there are a few examples of standing characters including the Hearty Good Fellow. Indeed, the Toby family developed considerably during the 1800s with the addition of the popular Punch and Judy, Woodman Toby – thought to have been modelled on British Prime Minister Gladstone – and Paul Pry, named after the play by John Poole. In 1934 Royal Doulton reintroduced the Toby Jug style in the form of character jugs, the first being John Barleycorn designed by Noke. Soon after followed a selection of Olde English and Dickensian characters and some were produced in great quantities. However, that has affected the value. A Dick Turpin jug, which was made from 1935 to 1960 was sold for £95 a couple of years ago. The second version which was in production until 1981 is unlikely to fetch more than half that figure. Other examples of the difference length of production can make to price include the Punch and Judy Man, made from 1964 to 1969, one of which has been sold for £360. On the other hand an Old Charley, which was in production for 45 years until 1983 went for only £42. A few Royal Doulton character jugs which were only in production for a short time will fetch as much as £1,000 with one, The Hatless Drake, being sold for £2,900 at auction a few years ago.

If your find looks less colourful than usual don't be too quick to dismiss it. Royal Doulton employees could buy 'seconds' which were left white. Collectors are keen to obtain these and at least £1,000 could be expected for such an example. Should it turn out to be an old white Toby then it probably dates from the eighteenth century but is generally not much sought after and is unlikely to fetch more than £100. Condition is always important with Toby Jugs and chips or cracks can halve their value. However, many avid collectors would rather have a damaged Georgian Toby than a pristine Victorian one, says Vic Schuler, so you may still get a fair price and it is certainly worth checking out.

Contacts

- Many books are available on the subject of Toby Jugs and the more recent character jugs. One of the best is British Toby Jugs by Vic Schuler published by Kevin Francis.

- Dealers are listed in publications like Exchange and Mart, but you might be better off contacting a large auction house such as Christie's first.

Unglazed (Biscuit) Figures

Changing fashions bring changing values and for some years there has been a move for the uncluttered look around people's homes. This has meant that previously valued items have been banished to attics, cupboards and drawers. Unfortunately some may even have been discarded completely. So as you look through those dusty hiding places you could well discover some of the colourful figures that used to adorn your mantlepieces and shelves. The fact that they were so popular does mean that there is plenty of choice for the would-be collector. High prices, therefore are only paid for the best examples or those that are particularly unusual.

In fact the 'big boys' of the auction and collectors world have paid scant attention to these delightful ornaments and there is little written material available to guide you through this world. Nor is there much indication on the figures themselves to show which particular factory produced them. However, most appear to have been made in Germany and France during the latter part of the nineteenth century and the early part of this century. They are made of a porcelain known as biscuit – popularly termed bisque, the French for biscuit – which has been fired once but then left unglazed. They are usually highly coloured.

One of the great attractions of these figures is that they are quite detailed though the intricate designs can be a problem in themselves since they leave the pieces prone to damage which will affect the price. Of course, a particularly unusual figure may still be of interest to a collector even if it is marred in some way but there are simply so many of these figures that it is unlikely a damaged piece will command much more than a few pounds. Biscuit porcelain figures fall into two basic groups. The first is pairs of figures in eighteenth century costumes very frequently dancing or paying court to each other. A pair of 13 inch French coloured biscuit figures in eighteenth century costume on mound bases were sold at a Christie's auction in 1987, together with another item, for £187. The second broad category is character figures, frequently children depicted in a doll-like way. One showing a little boy as a sailor with a small girl holding a shell to her ear, both sitting on a rock formation was sold for £220 at auction recently. It was delicately coloured and well modelled.

Collectors' interests often cross different barriers and this seems to be particularly true with these figures. Sporting characters attract considerable interest from those who seem to buy anything that has even the vaguest connection with sport. That may help to account for the near £200 price tag put on a pair of biscuit tennis players wearing blue and yellow Edwardian costumes when they were auctioned a year or so ago. Figures made in Russia tend to be less fancy than their European counterparts. They are much more rare and, if in perfect condition, will usually fetch a higher price. That was certainly the case with one example showing a pair of children playing musical instruments by a fence. It fetched £418 at Christie's in 1987.

An increasing number of these figures are being found and not all are of the finest quality. Both factors affect the prices so not all the figures tucked away in hidey-holes will be valuable. Children seated in armchairs are the most common that seem to be found and the price you'll get will reflect this. However, if you come across a really unusual figure you could be on to a real winner. An elaborately painted large Paris porcelain vase modelled with biscuit figures was included in an auction at Christie's in 1987. It sold for £792.

CHAPTER TWO:
CIGARETTE CARDS

In these days of Government Health warnings and bans on some advertising it is hard for the giant tobacco companies to come up with 'acceptable' ways to promote cigarette sales. Sponsoring different sports is one way to increase the public's awareness of particular manufacturers and their brands but perhaps they should think about going back to the 'gimmick' used by their predecessors more than fifty years ago: the free inserts known as cigarette cards.

For many of us the mere mention of the phrase cigarette cards will bring back memories of sitting in school playgrounds flicking them against a wall. Then the highest prices would be for the cards that were the strongest or would go the furthest. However, the intention of the manufacturers was to encourage smokers to collect the cards which meant buying the same brand over and over again.

Casting your memory back to school history lessons you'll recall that it was Sir Walter Raleigh in the sixteenth century who brought the first tobacco to England. Cigarettes were developed to make it easier for people to indulge in the smoking habit. However, there was only a fairly limited success until the end of the nineteenth century. The big boost came in the First World War when soldiers in the trenches found cigarettes were a way to calm their nerves. They continued to puff away when they returned home and smoking became common practice for people in all walks of life in the twenties.

By the 1930s collecting the cards given away free with every packet of cigarettes had become a real craze amongst schoolboys who used to hang around outside pubs, factory gates and theatres looking through the discarded cigarette packets in the hope of finding those few elusive cards that would mean they had a full set. Customers leaving tobacconists would find themselves pestered and it is only in more recent times that the idea of collecting the cards has caught on with adults – the original aim of the firms who gave them away.

However, because of the sheer numbers produced there is every chance of you coming across some when you are scouring through the attic or the secret hidey-hole where long forgotten treasures lurk. As with all such finds, many are worth little or nothing except as keepsakes. Indeed, in the days when they were issued by all the big tobacco firms there was never a real intention to create something of value. As I've said they were regarded as a way to promote sales but did provide a useful source of information. At a time when there was no television, cigarette cards were a wonderful way for people to view the world and what was happening in it. They were colourful and informative.

Cigarettes were originally sold by weight and the shopkeeper would put them in specially supplied envelopes or bags. Then they started to be supplied in flimsy paper packets. These were nothing like our 'crush proof' packs of today and left the contents vulnerable to being squashed. So the tobacco companies decided to include a piece of cardboard as a stiffener. This was back in the nineteenth century when tradesmen all had calling cards. These cards usually included some sort of advertisement for their products or services and were presented with their bill or across the counter in shops. The idea of 'trade' cards is thought to have come from France in the 1840s where shopkeepers hit on the idea of issuing sets of the cards, one a week, to encourage customers to return to the shop regularly.

Aristide Boucicaut, who founded Au Bon Marché in Paris is reckoned to be the first person to have come up with the idea of set of cards back in 1853. While other Continental countries took up the idea British tradesmen were less keen though it is still possible to find old business cards proclaiming the giver to be a 'purveyor of asses milk,' 'skeleton seller,' 'spadderdash and gaiter maker' and 'chimbley (sic) sweeper'. If there are any like this lurking in your Aladin's cave they are more likely to be of curiosity value than worth big money though some specialist collectors may be interested.

However, the card idea was brought to Britain and America in a slightly different form by manufacturers. Probably the best known is Liebig, the Oxo firm which in the hundred years from 1872 issued 2,000 different sets of cards to help promote their products. Subjects include the Trans-Siberian Railway, Shadowgraphs and even one of the life of the firm's founder Justus von Liebig. In the 1870s the early tobacco companies of Virginia hit on the idea of copying tradesmen and the manufacturers by printing the stiffeners in their cigarette packets with attractive pictures and informative text. However this was largely a form of advertising and well removed from what we now regard as the cigarette card.

One of the earliest American cards that has been discovered has a picture of the Marquis of Lorne, the some-time Governor of Canada, on it. It is thought to date from 1879. A year later the American firm Thos. W Hall produced a set of four presidential candidates and four actresses. Each of these cards is worth £40

Beauties of all Nations: Spanish; V.C. Heroes – Boer War; Miss Clara Cowper.
Source: Christie's.

today. By 1890 it is reckoned that almost every American tobacco firm had issued at least one series of cards, often of actresses.

Following this American lead, early British cards give a very good insight into the packaging and manufacture of cigarettes but little else. However, one card, thought to be a very early British example shows an 1884 calendar and details of United Kingdom postal rates. This fetched £510 nearly a decade ago and could now be worth double that – or even more. Before long the British firms followed their American competitors and produced cards with the faces of pretty girls. Many of these British cards were the product of American firms like Allen and Ginter which operated out of premises at London's Holborn Viaduct.

It is likely that the first truly British cigarette cards came from Wills with one well-known example showing a little boy running home from the tobacconists with the message "It's all right Father, 'tis Wills". It was probably also Wills who issued the first complete sets of true British cigarette cards in 1894 when they produced two series of 50 cards on soldiers and sailors, one with a blue background the other with grey. A complete set of either of these in good condition could be worth about £1,500 today with individual cards from the sets going for £30 each.

Victorian gentlemen had three major obsessions: imperial expansion, sport and buxom ladies. Not surprisingly they were all reflected in other early series. Players came out with a set of 25 of England's military heroes in 1898, each of which is currently valued at £20. Cope Bros came up with 52 beauties with playing card insert in 1899 which are probably worth about £25 each now and Marcus produced 25 footballers and club colours in 1898 presently valued at £60 each. Perhaps the most enterprising issue of this period came from Taddy with 20 cards in 1898 on royalty, actresses and soldiers. Each is now valued at £125.

One way of judging the age of cards from this period is to look at the history of the cigarrette firms. James Buchanan Duke whose American Tobacco Company had swallowed up some 250 smaller firms on the other side of the Atlantic decided he wanted to capture a chunk of the market in this country and coughed up over five million dollars for Ogden's of Liverpool, then one of the largest British tobacco firms. Their Guinea Gold cigarettes contained cards with real photographs and the Ogden's Tabs brand included black and white half-tones. In the four years from 1899 it is estimated that the firm issued more than 15,000 different cards with these brands alone. Not surprisingly, therefore, most of these cards are worth less than £1 each.

However, Duke was facing the combined strength of the British firms who joined forces to fight him off when they formed the Imperial Tobacco Company in 1901. As a result the old Wills cards had Imperial

Albert Hall; Up-to-date Tobacconist.
Source: Christie's.

Tobacco stamped on the reverse from 1902.

When the First World War put a temporary stop to cards in 1917 some 1,800 sets had been produced by 150 companies. However, the golden age of cigarette cards was still to come. In terms of numbers issued the period between the wars marked a high point, although many collectors claim the quality had deteriorated and this is reflected in the value of some later issues.

The large companies like Wills and Players issued a new set of cards every couple of months and had huge staffs of artists and writers working on them. Some were printed in enormous quantities like the 1936 collection of 50 Wills railway engines. Unbelievably there were 600 million of these published so they have little value today with a full set fetching no more than £15 even if in perfect condition.

One of the things that makes the cards of interest not only to collectors but for the rest of us as well is the way they reflected the social trends as the years went by. In the early days of the cards Victoria was still on the throne and we were still trying to protect the British Empire. Not surprisingly, therefore, the original issues concentrated on patriotic subjects. Cards were seen as a method of relaying news as the many series from the Boer War testify. Wills' Transvaal series is possibly one of the most

Union Jack of the Present; Spitfire.
Source: Christie's.

comprehensive with a total of 66 cards.One issue of these had a black border to mark the death of Victoria and these are worth about £5 each. However, there were also more frivolous issues with series on music hall stars, seaside resorts and prize fighters. That soon came to an end with the advent of the First World War when there was a return to military subjects.

Later on the cards were used to record the early days of flying, broadcasting and the cinema as well as such subjects as the centenary of the railways in 1925. There were sets of film stars of the day, cricket and football personalities, famous heroes and Dickens characters as well as birds, cars, planes, the rules of football, flags of the world and even palmistry – all on those little cards with a few words about the people and events on the back. One of the most popular subjects and one that is currently attracting a great deal of interest among collectors is cricket. While football fans tend to be interested in only the latest stars, cricket buffs have a deep sense of history and happily go back to W G Grace. He is featured in what was probably the first cricket set, the Wills series of 50 cricketers published in 1896. In good condition such a set would be worth around £2,000 today. Five years ago it would have been valued at less than £400.

In total about 350 tobacco manufacturers gave away cigarette cards before the Second World War and

The Language of Flowers and Heath; Sappho; H.R.H. the Prince of Wales.
Source: Christie's.

paper rationing put an end to the craze. The firms did not start re-issuing the cards after 1945 even though Carreras had the clever idea of printing the pictures on the trays of their Turf brand to save on paper. These were in two-tone blue and had nothing on the back and have become quite popular with collectors. Some series, like the 1950 famous cricketers are rare and can fetch as much as £50 a set, though the majority of post World War Two sets are unlikely to be worth much more than £15 and some as little as £3.50.

Cigarette cards have been issued in practically every country in the world at some time or another so there is a chance you might even find a foreign set tucked away. However, foreign cards are not as popular with collectors as the British ones so generally fetch less. Interestingly, the country of origin is often clearly reflected in the subject of cigarette card series. New Zealand firms were hot on natural history, Australian cards featured sport and the Germans published vast series which included such subjects as The Struggle For

40

Upper Sileasa and Robber State England.

Unlike postage stamps, printing errors detract from values rather than add to them and as these were common it is worth taking a close look before rushing off to a dealer or auction house with your find. However, there are some true rarities. A single card of a Clarke Tobacco Leaf Girl from 1898 is worth at least £250. No one is sure how many cards D & J Macdonald issued in its series cricket & football teams in 1902. So if you found one of them you could expect it to be worth at least £100.

War has also played its part in increasing the rarity of some sets and, therefore, their value. When Wills decided to issue a set of world musical celebrities it had not allowed for the problems of the First World War and the anti-German feelings it created in this country. It was forced to substitute eight cards featuring Germans or Austrians with less controversial, and less celebrated, musicians. Wills were also caught off-guard in the First World War because of a planned series on heroes from the Battle of Waterloo. This was produced in 1915 to commemorate the centenary of the battle but when it was realised that if might offend our French allies the cards were never issued. A few did escape from the printers, however, and these are now worth up to £1,000 a set.

It was also the Bristol based Wills that produced a series of cards illustrating the life of Edward VIII planned to be issued to tie in with his coronation. As Edward married Wallace Simpson he was never crowned and the cards were never issued. One of the first sets of these to be sold came from the private collection of William Wills, a great-great grandson of one of the founders of the firm. During the twenty-five years that he worked for the company he was given a set of every issue. He once claimed it was like a coin collector being let loose in the Mint. Mr Wills' set of the Edward cards fetched £200 back in 1973. Unfortunately several more sets have turned up since then and the set is now valued at around £40. The substitute set, Our King & Queen is worth even less, just £5 for all 50 in good condition.

Cards issued by the smaller tobacco firms generally attract more interest than those from the giant companies. Manufacturers whose cards are worth looking out for include W. Sandorides, Kinnear, Richmond Cavendish, F & J Smith of Glasgow, John Sinclair of Newcastle and James Taddy of London. Taddy went out of business because of a long labour dispute but in a final gasp before it expired in 1920 the firm issued a set of 20 clowns and circus artistes. It is thought that only 15 sets of this series exist and one of them fetched the staggering sum of £15,500 when put up for auction at Philips in 1987. Four years earlier a seller with 19 of the 20 cards in this series was given £4,200 for them. A single card is presently valued at £400. However, not all Taddy sets are worth a fortune. The somewhat less attractive Boer leaders series went for only £160 in 1987. The cheapest single Taddy card would probably fetch just a couple of pounds although each of the five cards produced by the company showing English royalty could be worth £300.

Generally, however, individual cards are not as interesting to collectors as a complete set – but here's hoping your relatives weren't the types addicted to glue. If they stuck them in an album or catalogue then they will be worth little or nothing.

Just how much your find will be worth depends on the rarity and condition of the cards. So if you discover one of the sets produced in millions during the 20s and 30s don't expect to have found a treasure. A few pounds is the most you are likely to get for them. Cigarette cards are only of interest to collectors if they

Kriegsfeld's Time; Beauty; Somali.
Source: Christie's.

have sharp edges and corners, are printed centrally on the card with the printing on the reverse clear and without errors. Marks or creases will reduce their value.

It is only in recent years that cartophily, to give cigarette card collecting its proper name, has really become popular. That accounts, in part, for the rising values. In the past ten years the most sought after series have nearly quadrupled in value. An annual guide to help you value any cards is produced by Murray Cards (International), and is the one used by most dealers and auction houses.

There are regular monthly magazines which can give you an indication about cards. Although most of the large auction houses have specialists who will value any finds either by post if you send a detailed description or personally so long as you make an appointment, you will probably do as well paying £4.95 for the Murray catalogue and doing the job for yourself. There are a couple of cigarette firms around the world who still produce the cards some of which

43

are reproductions of earlier issues and it is important not to confuse them with the originals.

Murray's can also help you with trade cards which have continued to be issued by all sorts of firms. Probably the most prolific has been Liebig whose series have covered everything from chess pieces to world's motorway. Full sets of their 1960s and 70s issues are worth a couple of pounds at the most. Tea firm Kardomah specialised in cards dealing with culture and each is worth around £2. Soap powder giant Lever Brothers were into patriotic series, sweets group Rowntrees issued cards showing local landmarks while rivals Barratt and Geo. Bassett have given away hundreds of different sets in their cigarette sweets over the years. Spratts the pet food firm was keen on sets showing dogs, the Typhoo Tea firm had some very interesting cards all about books and their rivals Brooke Bond covered natural history.

Originally these 'imitations' were not valued very highly but since 1970 they, too, have been in demand. The Typhoo Tea Animal Friends of Man series from 1927 is worth about £50 and a set of Oxo's 36 Lifeboats and Their History from 1935 is worth a little more. Don't forget demand, rarity and condition are still the ruling factors over what sets are worth. A 1967 series of 50 cards called Thunderbirds will probably fetch £50 while a similar set issued a year later would not be worth more than £5.

Breakfast cereal firms, newspapers and chewing gum manufacturers have all produced their own cards from time to time and these are also becoming popular. In 1966 American and British Gum produced several Batman cards. Full sets are worth between £22 and £50. Perhaps, the most unlikely source of cards was the local bobby. Kent Police distributed cards six years ago as a way of improving contact with young people. The set depicted England's World Cup Squad.

The South Wales Constabulary had the same idea only its set showed Welsh rugby stars. So far these are not of great value but given a few more years . . .

Summary

- Generally older cards are of more value than recent ones though in all cases the condition is important.
- Unlike stamps, errors in printing do not increase the value, rather the opposite.
- Full sets are usually of far greater value than just a few single cards from a series.
- Cards pasted into a book or in any way damaged so one side or the other is unclear are, on the whole, worthless.
- Magazines and collectors books are published which give guides to values.
- Don't send cards themselves through the post. Send a detailed description, including information on how many you have from each set. Alternatively take some photographs or photocopies of a few giving details of the rest.
- Use the Murray's catalogue as a way of valuing the cards for yourself.

Contacts

- Murray Cards (International), 51 Watford Way, Hendon Central, London NW4 3JH. Telephone 01-202 5688 produce the catalogue and will help with valuations and sales.

- Two main monthly magazines are produced: Cigarette Card Monthly, 15 Debdale Lane, Keyworth, Notts (£5.50) and Cigarette Card News & Trade Chronicle, Sutton Road, Somerton, Somerset (£9.50).

CHAPTER THREE:
COINS AND MEDALS

Everybody has old coins tucked away somewhere around the house. Pre-decimal coins were hastily stashed away when pound and pence were introduced in February 1971. For years people have hoarded pre-1946 silver coins – because they actually contained 50 per cent silver – and those from before 1920 have also been sought after since they are almost pure silver. Then, of course there are the millions of foreign coins tucked away in cupboards and drawers. They were left over after a holiday abroad and someone in the family thought they might be worth something someday. Sad to say most of the coins people find hidden away are not of any great value. Condition is of paramount importance as far as coins are concerned and, unless they are uncirculated – that is to say there are no marks or scratches at all – then most collectors are not interested. Obviously there are a few exceptions but not as many people seem to think.

First off let us lay to rest the theory about old silver coins. Clearly the value should reflect the amount of silver they contain. However, you would need a very large quantity of the metal to make it worth melting them down and, anyway, that is illegal. So you are left with the basic coin and its value to a collector will be determined both by its condition and how many were made. It was from the Roman silver coin dinarius that Britain got the 'd' in '£ s d' – the old currency. Based on the Roman's ideas about coinage, Saxon Britain developed several different coins so that by the time William the Conqueror landed most towns around the country were minting their own coins, which were silver pennies. The Normans had very little influence on coins and so for some 700 years the silver penny – not always looking very attractive as in the case of the grotesque King John ones – survived wars, plague and revolution.

A change took place in 1797 when Matthew Boulton's 'cartwheels' were introduced – the first copper two pence pieces and pennies. Today one in poor condition would cost a few pounds but if it is unmarked in any way then you might get as much as £80. Bronze pennies came into use in 1860 with Queen Victoria's famous bun-head issue which lasted 33 years. Along the way there were many 'specials' like the six known Henry III gold pennies. One hundred years ago one of these would have been worth a little over £200. In June 1985 one was sold at auction for £65,000. Obviously coins of such vintage are rare and the best examples are already in museums. These are not the sort of coins you will just come across in an attic or cupboard, and if you do discover one it is a genuine 'find'.

Most likely you will find coins minted since the middle of the last century when the first steps towards decimalisation were taken. A silver florin, equal to one tenth of a pound and our present day 10p piece – was issued for the first time in 1849. Half crowns were temporarily withdrawn – returning in 1984. Queen Victoria's Golden Jubilee was marked by new style gold and silver coins, there was a special sixpence and for just four years a double florin was produced. Another redesign took place in 1893 when the portrait of Victoria was changed on gold and silver coins but it was not included on bronze coins until 1895.

There was one major mint in London but also some other mints around the country and so some coins have marks on them to show where they were produced. This will affect the value as will any note of a die number on the coin. High value coins like sovereigns and half sovereigns do not always command the highest prices. Few early Victorian sovereigns are worth more than £150 in tip top condition, much the same price as you will get for many half sovereigns. Crowns were less common and so even a slightly worn one from the 1840s is likely to fetch at least £16. And you can get a fiver for a halfcrown from 1880 that's showing considerable signs of wear. A shilling worth looking out for would be one from 1850. Even a worn one could be worth £90. However, most worn shillings will only fetch a couple of pounds and you'll probably not get more than £1 for a worn Victorian sixpence. Strangely enough the Victorian threepenny piece is more likely to be worth a few pounds as are some of the pennies and halfpennies. For some reason most people who come across coins seem to think it is the farthing that is worth money. Partly because of its original value and because of the number produced this is simply not true. With a few exceptions they must be in what is officially called 'very fine condition' to be worth anything and even then it's only likely to be a couple of pounds.

As we mentioned earlier: condition is important. Experts refer to 'fine' when they mean it shows some signs of wear, though this should not have badly damaged the design, 'very fine' when they mean it has only been in limited circulation and 'extra fine' when it shows little or no sign of ever having been circulated. Most of the pennies, halfpennies and farthings issued in the latter part of Victoria's reign would need to be extra fine to command any value at all. Edward VII bronze coins also need to be in extra fine condition to

The Louis XIII gold coin that sold for £61,600 at Christie's on 6th October 1987. Called the Quatre Louis d'Or, it is one of only seven examples struck and was used exclusively at the French King's gaming table. Source: Christie's.

be worth anything and few circulated silver coins command more than a couple of pounds.

George V halfcrowns, florins and shillings in extra fine condition may fetch £10 or so, sixpences are worth around £10 in the same state while threepenny pieces are unlikely to be worth more than a couple of pounds. Pennies vary in price depending on the year and the markings. Certain 1926 ones in uncirculated condition might be worth £500 while others would not fetch more than £35. However, the most rare is a 1933 penny. Even in mint condition halfpennies and farthings from George V's reign are unlikely to fetch more than £10 with most valued at less than a fiver. No coins were generally issued with Edward VIII's portrait but a couple did come up for auction in 1984/85. A sixpence went for £9,500 and a sovereign fetched £40,000.

The more recent the coin the less likely you are to find a collector interested in anything other than one in uncirculated condition. Thus even a fairly rare 1938 shilling is only worth a couple of pounds if it shows any signs of having been used. Most halfcrowns, florins, shillings and sixpences even uncirculated will only be worth £5 to £10 if produced in the latter part of George VI's reign. Much the same is true of the coins bearing our present Queen's head though florins from 1954, 1957 and 1959 may bring £20 to £30 if uncirculated. One coin many people collected – and that in itself has affected the value – is the Churchill crown issued in 1965. In perfect condition it is still worth only 75p.

Some Elizabeth II coins to look out for include 1957 and 1959 Scottish style shillings and 1958 English style shillings all of which are worth around £15 in tip top condition. Threepence pieces from before 1960 are valued at up to £5. A 1954 penny would be extremely rare. Decimal coins need to be in proof sets to have any interest for collectors and even then you won't be looking at more than two times face value in most cases. Fake coins have turned up from time to time though the best of these command their own collectors' value. These are eighteenth century forgeries of ancient coins by Karl Becker who used a metal box fitted to the back axle of his carriage to 'age' his counterfeits.

In amongst the foreign coins you might discover tucked away somewhere could be some American ones. These usually have some value even if they are slightly worn provided they date from 1790 to 1810. For example, a 1795 cent even quite well worn could fetch £100 and if in better condition it might be worth several hundred. American copper tokens from the eighteenth century are valued at up to £5. Coins from other countries, if from either the eighteenth or nineteenth century, are worth checking out with an expert or by looking in one of the many catalogues kept at local libraries. However, if it is just bits and pieces of holiday money from the past thirty years or so then it simply isn't worth the effort.

Do's and Don'ts'

- Don't try to clean old coins. You may damage the surface and so reduce the value.

- Do check values with catalogues or several dealers before accepting an offer.

- Do make sure any dealer is a member of the British Numismatic Trade Association – BNTA.

- Don't expect to get the catalogue value for your coins. That is the price the dealers will charge. You are unlikely to get more than half to two-thirds of that price.

- Do go to an auction house if you have very old coins or any worth large amounts. They will probably get a better price for you than you'll get through a dealer though, of course, you will have to pay commission and VAT.

• Don't hoard badly damaged or well worn coins from the last 100 years or so. They aren't worth much now and don't look likely to increase in value in the near future.

Summary

Old British copper coins are unlikely to be of great value, especially those from this century, with the notable exceptions of the 1950/51 pennies and the 1933 penny. However, all the 1933 pennies are thought to have been accounted for so if you find one check it is not a fake. Silver coins since 1946 are generally not worth much though those between 1920 and 1946 – which contained 50 per cent silver – should reflect the value of the silver. The same goes for those minted before 1920, which should be worth twelve times their face value on the basis of their silver content.

However, remember that condition is important to collectors and, as no one is likely to be looking at the melt-down value, this is the over-riding factor in determining worth. Gold coins are always worth something and should be carefully checked out. A reputable jeweller or coin dealer will help and in the case of gold coins will probably give you up to 90 per cent of the value. Auction houses are good for older coins but the big dealers like Spink & Son or Seaby are the places to go to check out more recent issues.

Contacts

Spink & Son, 5 King Street, London SW1.
01-930 7888.

Seaby, B A Ltd, 8 Cavendish Square, London W1.
01-631 3707.

Regular magazines include Coin Monthly, Coin Weekly, Coin and Stamp Fair News, Coins and Medals, and Coin Market Values.

Medals

Headline grabbing newspaper stories about people cashing in their old medals and coming away with vast sums of money have awakened a great deal of interest in this area. It has also encouraged more people to search out the awards given to their family's heroes and put them up for sale. When there is a glut of most 'collectibles' it results in lower prices. While this may be true for the more general medals, it is not the case for the most part. This is because medals have a major edge over stamps, coins and paper money – areas to which they are frequently linked by popular newspaper writers. With medals you get personal identification: usually the recipient's name, rank and regiment or the ship. A little investigative work and, especially if the person who originally received the medal was an officer, you can build up a fairly full dossier on the event, the people involved, and the recipient of the particular medal you have.

As far as we can tell the first British award for courage went to Sir Robert Welch in 1642. It marked his success at rescuing the standard at Edge Hill. Most early awards were given to people who were involved in naval encounters like the defeat of the Spanish Armada. Admirals and commanders who took part in that gallant venture were given the Ark in Flood medal by Queen Elizabeth I. It was made of gold and silver and intended to be worn round the neck. However, Drake's medal, which was personally awarded to him by the Queen, was somewhat different. It featured a cameo cut in onyx which was set with diamonds and rubies. The other side shows the date – 1581 – and a miniature by Nicholas Hilliard.

First of the campaign medals was the one for people who fought at the battle of Dunbar, 1650, and the next was for those who were at Waterloo and was issued in 1815. Today such a medal would be worth at least £150. Queen Victoria introduced the Military General Service Medal in 1848 but it was backdated and awarded to people who had taken part in battles since 1793 and who were still around to collect it – which many weren't! Although medals have continued to be issued throughout the years they are still relatively limited in number – certainly when compared with coins – and so are more highly prized by collectors.

Prices do depend on the engagement involved, the part played by the recipient, and whether that person was famous in any other way or became a particular hero whose story was widely told. A Military General Service medal with two clasps for the Borneo and South Arabia confrontations would normally be worth around £40. However, when one came up for sale a short time ago it was discovered that the recipient had been an SAS trooper and was killed in action. As a result the final price paid was £950. There's a good market for the Victoria Campaign and Gallantry medals and a Victoria Cross will fetch at least £6,000. However, the final price could be many times that if there is sufficient interest in the particular award. That is one of the reasons why medals are often best suited to the auction room. A dealer will be making a judgement on how much he can re-sell it for and will tend to err on the low side. At an auction the publicity might well arouse interest from museums, the regiment to which the recipient belonged or the families of others involved in the battle. So a higher price, while not guaranteed, will often be achieved.

The Military Medal, issued to the army for particular actions during the First World War will be worth at least £40 while the Distinguished Conduct

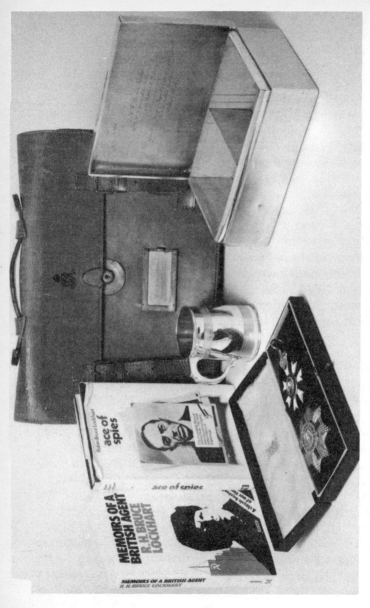

KCMG, Christening mug, attache case and silver cigar box belonging to R. H. Bruce Lockhart. Sold at Christie's in London on July 19th, 1988 for £13,000.

Medal, also issued to the army during the First World War will fetch at least £100. Remember these are only STARTING prices – you may well get a lot more. When you are rummaging around in the attic be careful not to separate relevant bits and pieces. Groups of medals, the documents that went with them, photos and any other related material will add to the value. A gallantry medal is often worth a great deal when it can be presented with other medals that relate to it.

Naval Distinguished Service medals from the First World War will bring upwards of £120 at auction; the Distinguished Service Order medal is likely to fetch at least £200 and you can expect more than £250 if the medal you find is the Distinguished Service Cross which was issued to naval officers for acts of gallantry. Campaign medals can also be of value. Those from the Crimea will bring in at least £50 and those from the Falklands are currently worth around £70, though as more and more come onto the market the price is tending to drift downwards. As people leave the service they are cashing in their medals since it is illegal to do so while you are still serving. Not all medals you find will be worth selling, though. General campaign medals from the First and Second World Wars are of very little value, again since there were so many of them. Civilian awards will, usually, bring high prices if offered at auctions. A George Medal should be worth upwards of £350, a George Cross exchange – that is one issued in exchange for the Albert Medal – should fetch at least £1,000 and an ordinary George Cross will start at around £2,000.

In the case of most finds you might make, the recommendation is to take a photograph and let the auction house or dealer use that to give you a round guide as to the value. That is not so easy with medals. All the details – like those that might be on accompanying documents, together with the name of the recipient are needed to give a proper valuation. You can, of course, write all that down and send it off, but you would usually be better telephoning for guidance or making a personal visit taking the medal with you.

CHAPTER FOUR:
FINANCIAL BITS AND PIECES

Millions of pounds are sitting around in the vaults of banks, building societies and insurance companies as well as government coffers just waiting to be claimed by their rightful owner. Some of it could be yours. As you rummage around in the attic or those drawers where so many old keepsakes are to be found it will be easy to spot most of the things we've talked about in this book. However, lots of folk are 'blind' to pieces of paper: the mere thought of anything connected with money or the world of finance and they drop whatever it is like a hot cake. Yet it may be very simple to turn that old yellowed scrap into crinkly fivers, tenners or twenty pound notes. All you have to know is what to do with what you find. Obviously if it is connected with your own affairs then you'll have a very good idea, though you may be surprised to learn that lots of folk don't even keep track of their own finances. The biggest problem is moving house. Papers are often bundled up together with an elastic band and then just thrown to the back of a drawer as soon as the unpacking begins. The new address is not passed on to the people who need to know.

Take dear old Ernie. There is £5,550,000 in unclaimed premium bond prizes waiting to be handed out. National Savings go to great lengths to try and track down the owners of winning bonds but even they draw a blank occasionally. The starting point is the address they were originally given. From there the trail can lead to the jungles of the Amazon where one lucky winner was found. Another search ended in a Monastery but some, inevitably lead to a dead end. If you do come across some old premium bonds which you think may have been winners you can always find out by checking the special supplement to the *London Gazette*. You should find a copy in main post offices or at some libraries. Above all else make sure that you write to the Bonds and Stock Office, Government Buildings, Lytham St Annes, FY0 1YN and let them know where you are now living. That is also the address to write to if the bonds you've found belonged to a relative who has now popped their clogs. So long as you can prove that you are the person who inherited you'll be able to get the money back – as well as any unclaimed prizes.

Your main post office should be able to help if your 'find' is some other form of National Savings and you are not sure how to go about getting your money back. Probably the most likely thing you'll come across is an old post office savings book. This has since been turned into the National Savings ordinary account. It may sound unbelievable but around £196 million is tied up in these accounts in one form or another and has not been touched for at least five years. In some cases it has been lying there for between forty and fifty years. One explanation is that young foreign fighters who joined Britain during the last war opened accounts but were sadly never to return and collect the cash. They had no relatives to even know that the cash was there. Even some of our own heroes may not have told their loved ones about the savings and so the money is doomed to sit waiting for someone who will never return to claim it. There must be some old books lying around in homes up and down the country, however. If there is more than £1 in the account then its also been clocking up interest so there might be quite a tidy sum waiting to be collected. Not for the author though, I'm afraid. My old post office savings book has just a couple of shillings in it but it would still be sensible for me to have that transferred to a new National Savings ordinary account. If I want to do that I need to contact National Savings Bank, Boydstone Road, Glasgow G58 1SB.

Earlier we mentioned the war and there is another stash of money dating back to those dark days which is waiting to be collected by the patriotic folk who have either forgotten about it or don't realise it's there. Soldiers, workers and their families were given Post War credits at the height of the Second World War when tax allowances were cut. After the war these could be cashed in once the holders reached retiring age. At that time 17,000,000 taxpayers could claim a total of £765 million. Many forgot to collect their cash so between 1959 and 1972 the government added interest to what was owed. That encouraged a few more of the credits to be unearthed. There are still 2,000,000 people who have not staked their claim, however, and there is £46,368,000 – including the extra interest – sitting in the government's coffers waiting for the rightful owners. Nor do you have to be past retirement age to collect. In many cases, of course, the original owner has died and the credits may have been lost. However, so long as the Post War credit certificates are still around then the money can be claimed. If you find such a certificate you'll need to get a repayment form from: Post War Credits, Inspector of Taxes, PWC Centre, Ty Glas, Llanishen, Cardiff CF4 5TX. Send it back with the certificates and the cash is yours.

Banks and building societies are generally reluctant to admit just how much money they've got their hands on which looks unlikely to ever find its way back to the

Pearl Life Policy for sum assured of £50. Annual premium £2 16s 8d. Dated 1899.

rightful owner. Barclays, NatWest, Midland and Lloyds all suggest that 'a few million' may be in accounts which have not been used for five years or more, which they refer to as 'dormant'. When they got rid of old pass books which people kept to show them how much they had tucked away for a rainy day, the banks put everything onto computer. Since some folk have cash which, for one reason or another, they are reluctant to let the taxman know about, this meant some customers had no official record of their secret hoard at home. If you do come across an old pass book it is worth checking out whether the cash is still there – though you must remember it could have been withdrawn since computerisation and that would not show up on the pass book. However, TSB England and Wales do admit that there's about £40 million tucked away in accounts with them that has not been touched for years. So long as you can prove that you are either the original owner or the person who is legally entitled to inherit then you can collect and the local branch will help. Much the same applies to building societies, who also decline to admit just how much money is tied up in dormant accounts. So never discard any old savings books and approach the bank or building society as if you are convinced that the cash is still there and you have a right to it.

Insurance companies also make a fortune out of folk who are lazy or unorganised. It is reckoned that every year thousands of claims against life assurance policies fail to be made either because people don't realise that they are entitled or because the person who took out the policy has left papers in such a mess that no one comes across the relevant documents. According to big firms like the Pearl and the Pru, many of the policies are the old 'penny' policies. These were taken out by people years ago as a way to cover funeral expenses. However, the few shillings a year they paid never

Pearl Infantile Policy plus premium receipt book. 1907.

really amounted to anything. Letters to the *Mirror* often complain about just this. The relative has come across a policy which has been paid for fifty or more years and is upset to find the payout is only around £20 when the claim is made. Still it is better than nothing and you should certainly write to the insurance firm about any policy you unearth. If you have difficulty in tracking down the company who issued the policy – they may well have moved or merged with another firm – then contact the Association of British Insurers, Aldermary House, Queen Street, London EC4N 1TT who should be able to tell you the new name or address.

Another piece of paper that you may find tucked away is a share or unit trust certificate. According to the people who keep the registers of folk who own shares and unit trusts, millions of certificates are reported lost or stolen every year and replacements issued. So there is a good chance that the one you come across may have been replaced, even so it is worth finding out. Most certificates have the name of the company on them – or the unit trust firm – and the registrars (the people who keep the register of holders). A letter to either of these should help to establish whether you have a valuable find or a worthless piece of paper.

In the case of a share certificate, if the registrar's name is not on it and you can find no trace of the company then a trip to the library is your next move. Have a look in the Stock Exchange Official Year Book to see if the firm has moved to a new address. There is also a publication called 'Who Owns Whom' where you will be able to track down the company if it has been taken over provided it still trades under its old name. Of course, if you have a broker – or maybe even your bank manager – then you could ask them to try and track down details. You might find a bigger bonus than you expect. As we mentioned earlier people forget to pass on their change of address and this could mean that there are dividends which have been paid on the shares but never collected because the company cannot find out where to send them. The giant Shell oil firm has £4.6 million waiting for elusive shareholders. British Telecom say that 65,000 people haven't collected their dividends during the past three years while the TSB is sitting on nearly £1 million of unclaimed shareholders' cash.

Whatever happens do not be scared to ask about any bits of paper that you find tucked away and which you don't understand. If they are not worth anything it doesn't matter but they just might turn out to be worth a great deal.

CHAPTER FIVE:
GLASS

You would have to go back around 5,000 years if you wanted an original piece of glass since the art of glassmaking is reckoned to have originated in Western Asia about 3,000 BC. The invention of the blowpipe around 300 BC led to a great expansion in glass-making. You'll find plenty of examples in museums and exhibitions around the world. It was the Venetians who, through the ages were regarded as the greatest glass makers but it took an Englishman, George Ravenscroft – who lived from Ravenscroft – who lived for 1618 to 1681 – to come up with a revolution in glassmaking. He added a special ingredient, an oxide of lead called litharge. This made the glass heavy but even more brilliant, reflecting light much as a diamond does.

History played its part in the development of glass in the eighteenth century when Jacobite glasses were used to drink the health of the Young Pretender. Such glasses are adorned with symbols like a rose, an oak leaf, a thistle, a portrait of one of the Pretenders, verses from Jacobite ballads, royal crowns, stars, the cipher J. R. for James Rex plus the number 8 and a message. Those with the message Amen are called Amen glasses and are the most treasured of all Jacobite glasses. However, they are also the ones that have been most forged over the years. They were made from 1747 for a small group of Jacobite hierarchy and have verses of Jacobite hymns engraved on them ending with the word Amen. Just as valuable are the Williamite glasses thought to have been made for the fiftieth anniversary of the Battle of the Boyne. These have engravings of an Irish harp, an Orange Order toast, a reference to the Boyne and, possibly, William on horseback.

It was a tax that finally hit this sort of glass. It was introduced in 1745 and was based on the weight. As a result the lead content was reduced and facet cutting on anything but the stems came to an end being replaced by engraving on the new, thinner glass. However, the Irish took until 1825 to introduce the levy and that has helped to push up the value of the Waterford glass produced in the intervening years. When the bridge across the Tyne was opened in 1796 the event was marked by the introduction of the celebrated Sunderland glasses, which later commemorated naval victories as well. Today one of these can fetch as much as £200, though the older the example the greater the price generally.

With the removal of the tax on glass in 1845 the beautifuly engraved glasses faced competition from the Bohemian coloured glass. In the early part of the nineteenth century English coloured glass centered mainly on the popular Bristol blue and green in traditional designs – a set of three decanters from this period were sold in 1987 for £420 and a single English green fluted wine glass fetched £43. However, towards the end of the 1800s the influence of the Bohemian arists could be seen. Some even came to live in England which benefited factories in Stourbridge such as Richardson and Bacchus & Sons. An English doughnut shaped decanter and stopper, thought possibly to have been made by Webb around the middle of the nineteenth century was sold for £320 in 1985. One of the biggest influences that the Bohemians had was in cased or overlay glass and opaline glass. By the middle of the nineteenth century England was competing strongly with Bohemia in the production of all sorts of overlay items from beakers and vases to scent bottles and decanters. A white and frosted scent bottle was sold at Christie's for £500 in June 1988.

It was the French who became the experts with opal, opaline or opalescent glass. As its name implies this glass looks a little like the gemstone. A large French opaline baluster-shaped vase from the mid-nineteenth century sold for £900 at auction in September 1988. Unusual items from this period like rolling pins, walking sticks and bells made by Nailsea with swirls of colour in them were attractive and are still sought after. Rare examples can fetch quite good money at auction.

Not only did the English glassmakers take on board the Bohemian ideas and designs but they also adopted and adapted ideas from all over Europe and the result was some fine Victorian decorative glass. The most distinctive is cranberry glass which was used to make everything from sugar bowls and plates to drinking glasses and centrepieces. One of the latter came up for auction at Christie's in 1987 and was sold for £280. The quality of items produced in coloured glass in the latter part of the nineteenth century deteriorated with a lack of detail in the engraving. The cheaper and quicker idea of staining in colours was introduced giving more of a feel of mass-production. This brought glass items within the reach of the masses but that is a fact reflected in prices paid by collectors. However, an English ruby-stained posy holder from this style still managed to fetch £65 when it was auctioned in 1988. Rock crystal was introduced to meet the Victorian demand for deeply engraved, highly polished sparkling glass. A combination of William Morris and Philip Webb resulted in the elegant wine glasses and tumblers

Lalique frosted glass vase, 6¼ inches high, acid etched.
R. Lalique, France. Sold 29 July 1988 for £495.
Source: Christie's.

of the period which were the forerunners of today's best examples.

Judging for yourself the age of glass is difficult but possible. The higher the lead content the older the glass is likely to be and the darker it will appear. Original Waterford glass is very greyish. Old glasses should also have a large roughened punty or pontil mark on the base. You should also be able to see lots of scratches showing that it has been lowered onto a table many times. On a genuinely old glass these scratches will be very irregular but if you examine them under a magnifying glass and they have some sort of regular pattern then you can be sure the glass is a fake. Use will also have damaged the edges of the design on engraved glasses. One way to fix the date of a glass is by examining the shape of the stem, the bowl and the feet. However, it needs an expert eye to do this successfully. You might find books on the subject – see below – will help for many include a dating chart and detailed explanations of such terms as Ratafias and Rummerts, annulated and cushion knobs on stems, balustroid and silesian stems, ogee, trumpet and bell bowls and beehive, domed or stepped feet.

While everybody knows that good glass 'rings' or 'sings' when gently flicked with the finger or when the finger is gently rubbed around the rim, experts do not suggest this is the best thing for the average person to do – accidents do happen! Glass really is an area where expert advice is needed but please don't take that as a cue not to bother and to start using those 'unusual' glasses grandma kept for everyday purposes. Full sets are often worth a lot more than individual glasses and chips and cracks can reduce values – though not always.

Along with any glasses you may find tucked away in the attic or the back of the sideboard in an old house may be a decanter or two. Again damage will reduce

A 'Lynn' carafe, 10 inches high. Sold 19 September 1988 at Seend Green House Sale for £495. (Left) An unusual 'Lynn' mallet shaped decanter, 11 inches high. Sold 19 September 1988 at Seend Green House for £352.

the value and it may not always be apparent. Since many decanters are heavy 'worked' the design can hide small chips and general wear and tear. The stopper may also affect the price if it is not the original one. A heavily cut, shaft and globe necked Victorian decanter can be worth around £70 with that acting as a starting point for those in good condition from earlier dates. Other glass items can also be of value. Heavy cut glass ashtrays can fetch up to a tenner on market stalls and you might get twice that or more for interesting items like vinaigrettes and silver-ended scent bottles and inkwells. A real find would be something made of Galle glass. Emile Galle lived in Meisenthal between 1846 and 1904 and gained a reputation for copying the art forms of medieval Europe and Japan. He also made glasses like the Jacobite ones with verses engraved on them. A Galle cameo vase might be worth as much as £550, while one of his perfume burners would be expected to go for £1,000. Many of his pieces were signed by Galle himself.

Louis Comfort Tiffany was a contemporary and the trans-Atlantic equivalent of Galle. Characteristics of his work include peacock feathers, leaves and Japanese style patterns frequently in his own patented iridescent glass. Tiffany was often copied by others, most notably J Lotz Witwe of Klostermuhle. A genuine Tiffany piece will fetch at least £500 and his lamps can reach as much as £10,000 at auction. Another name to watch out for is Rene Lalique whose elegant smokey glass, large plates, bowls and vases with naked nymphs and waving reeds are much collected.

One area of glassware that often catches the attention of writers – and some experts – is paperweights. Age and condition will play their usual part in the value along with the originator. Clichy and Baccarat are two names to look out for with a Baccarat butterfly and wheat flower weight fetching £4,104 at a 1986 auction. A modern candlestick paperweight brought in just £28 in 1987 at the same time as six Stourbridge paperweights went for £55.

CHAPTER SIX:
POSTCARDS

Somehow picture postcards seem terribly English but it was actually the Austrians who invented the idea back in 1869. The Paris Exhibition in 1889 gave a big boost to the idea of sending postcards but they were still not permitted in Britain. In fact our post office refused to accept them until 1894 when it was decided that it would be all right so long as the back of the postcard was given over entirely to the address and half of the front was used for the message – limiting the picture to the other half. Early British cards were smaller than their continental counterparts but in 1889 the post office eventually agreed to fall in line with the bigger size. In 1902 the divided back was permitted so that the message and address were on one side leaving the other entirely for the picture. These cards were mass produced in Saxony which accounted for the production for the whole world market.

Postcards were then sold in Britain for a halfpenny each which remained the second class postage rate until the end of the First World War. Indeed the period between 1902 and 1914 has been called the Golden Age of picture postcards when almost every conceivable subject was pictured. This led to a craze for postcard collecting similar to that enjoyed by cigarette cards with almost every boy and girl having an album of their own. Some early postcards commemorate such things as the death of Verdi and the assassination of King Humbet. The list of subjects was endless, from Father Christmas, Freaks and Fire Engines to Pigs, Pretty Ladies and Political figures. One of the most popular series from the early part of this century was the London Life cards produced by Rotary Photographic. These are worth at least £10 and some may fetch as much as £40 each.

One thing that helped postcards to catch on was the personal endorsement by Prime Minister Gladstone. Much as companies today believe that getting famous people to recommend their products helps boost sales so Gladstone's views encouraged others to use this convenient form of sending postal messages. Of course, these were the days before telephones and picture postcards were looked on as the cheapest and most reliable form of communication. By the First World War there were 50 million being mailed every week and most were being printed in Germany. Obviously, that changed and many cards were produced during the struggles featuring patriotic and military subjects. In addition, troops would often send cards home to wives and sweethearts. It would be normal to expect at least £25 each for such momentos and up to £10 more depending on the quality and condition. However, there are also embroidered and silk cards from this period and these can be worth considerably more.

The end of the war did not see postcards returning to their former prominent position. The telephone was becoming much more commonplace, the cost of postage was doubled and companies were, anyway, in difficulties. Also, most people had suffered great personal tragedies and so were in no mood for the lighthearted postcards that had been the rage earlier in the century. Of course, the 'wish you were here' style card has always remained popular and quite large numbers of cards were produced showing local views. These are generally not that highly valued unless there are particularly interesting aspects to them – like people where there would be interest in their style of clothing. Perhaps the most famous postcards are those featuring the work of Louis Wain – the funny catman – and Raphael Kirchner and, of course, our own Donald Magill whose saucy postcards have been popular for years and copied and embellished as people's tolerance of 'naughty' subjects has increased. Another favourite is Mabel Lucy Attwell whose childrens' cards have delighted people for years.

Collectors are always keen to get hold of postcards featuring pin-ups, society beauties and actresses. However, for the really big money you'll need to find the Art Nouveau style where those featuring the work of people like Alphonse Mucha can be worth up to £100 and you could get £500 or more for a Lautrec card. In these cases, of course, you really need to contact an auction house where a single card may fetch a much higher price than by going direct to a collector or a specialist shop. A special balloon card went for £1,000 not so long ago when put up for auction. However, ordinary views of streets, churches, cathedrals and monuments are very unlikely to be worth money. Shops will probably give you a few pence each if you are lucky and the cards are in good condition. Stations and trains do tend to be of greater

77

Selection from Printed Ephemera Sale on 27 October 1988. Prices realised between £770 and £120. Source: Christie's, South Kensington.

78

interest particularly if the line in question no longer exists – at least Beeching can be credited with some beneficial effect! Other transport and vehicle pictures will also bring in a few pounds.

If you come across a postcard album then it is unlikely to contain a real gem – but don't just discard it. Experts IPM say one in ten cards in such albums may be of some interest and make the exercise of valuing them worthwhile. However, if they are stuck down that can be a big minus point since there are a number of people interested in postal history for whom the postmark may be important. There were travelling post offices and also some stations were allowed to frank their own stamps and this could turn an otherwise valueless card into one worth up to £100. A prime example would be one sent from the Titanic. If the postmark showed that it was posted on board then the sky is virtually the limit. Even ordinary cards of the ship fetch up to £25.

To be of value a card should be as clean as possible on the front (picture side). It is permissible to use a very soft rubber but if you are in any doubt it is better to leave well alone rather than destroy what might be valuable. In addition there should be no pin holes. Some collectors, as well as being interested in the postal history, also seem to have a prying mind. So they are more than happy to buy postcards with messages written on them. Used or unused, then, they can be worth money. This is one case where sending a photograph to someone for a valuation does not really help and you will need to contact a member of the Postcard Traders Association to find out what your find is worth. Most local libraries have catalogues which will give you some idea about values and give you contacts for dealers. In addition there are frequent local fairs plus the monthly get together at the Bloomsbury Fair where there are regularly 150 tables set up with collectors and dealers. It is held at the Royal National Hotel, Woburn Place, London WC1.

Contacts

- Probably the most comprehensive catalogue is the one from IPM Publications, PO Box 190, Lewes, Sussex BN7 1HF. It is priced at £7.50.

- There is also a two monthly guide to local sales and monthly guide to local sales and happenings which costs £3.50 a year from Top Table Promotions, 18a Bell Lane, Hendon, London NW4, the London address for IPM.

- Stanley Gibbons and most big auction houses have experts who can help you identify and value your find.

- There are also several magazines on the subject. The leading British publication is Picture Postcard Monthly.

London Life. 'Votes for Women'.

London Life. The Brewer's Man. (Universally hailed an indispensable type.)

CHAPTER SEVEN:
RECORDS

Most people build up a record collection without ever really thinking about it. As families grow up the different stages are reflected in the music that's bought and when one era is over the records are cast aside, but often no further than the attic or junk room.

A peek into the treasure trove will reveal a lot of old memories. Blow off the dust and they can be relived in a moment providing your modern hi-fi can play old scratched 45s, LPs or, even less likely, 78s. Sad to say, until the fairly recent arrival of the compact disc, those memories will have aged and be accompanied by inevitable scratches, cracks and clicks.

Those are the things that could well reduce the value of your hoard to nothing. The scratches are not inevitable – just commonplace. Most young record buyers took their latest purchases to parties and friends' houses sharing the pleasure with others, often on a Dansette record player with a sapphire stylus and a pick-up weighing ten times more than today's models. However, there were people who kept their records in covers, not loose in wire 'toast racks', handled them with care and played them on good stereograms. Such people are few and far between but if someone in your family was like that you may find some diamonds in your collection.

Of course, a member of your family may also have been 'in the business' either as a rep or a dealer. These are the people whose collections will prove the most valuable as they are quite likely to have 'demos' – promotional copies of records along with other publicity material. Also, the records may well have never been played, just simply tucked away.

Little did Thomas Edison realise what he was starting when he shouted: "Mary had a little lamb . . ." into his new-fangled phonograph back in 1877. Indeed it's said he could see no future in his invention and could not be bothered to develop it until competition came along.

Even then he persisted with cylinders though they were now based on wax instead of the original tin foil. The result was very poor quality but, surprisingly, they remained popular right into the twenties. Those old cylinders can be of value so if your attic has been untouched for years and you find a hoard of them you must seek out an expert. The big auction houses will be happy to point you in the right direction and you may even find that the special museums of recorded history will be interested in adding your find to their own collection, though like the recently formed National Sound Archives they will not generally pay for contributions. Better still if you find a player. These are real antiques and collectors will pay large sums for them.

However, it was Edison's rival Emile Berliner, who was born in 1851, who really started the records spinning. You might say he put everyone in a flat spin, for he was the man who introduced the flat record and the gramophone.

It was his first earlier invention, the microphone – bought by Alexander Graham Bell for use with the telephone – that gave Berliner the money to work on his project. Even then he had to take the idea back to his native Germany – he had emigrated to the States when he was 19 – to get the finance to turn his ideas into a product. The plates, as they were called, were first exhibited to the public in June 1888 and ten years later the Gramophone company started up in London's Maiden Lane. Its first artist was a soprano who sang next door in Rules restaurant.

By now a clockwork mechanism had been added to the gramophone so the sound heard was much closer to what had been recorded since the motor had a governor fitted which regulated the speed.

Much of the music of that period was opera so it is not surprising that the first million selling record was of Enrico Caruso singing Vesti La Giubba (On With The Motley).

The history of records, once they had established themselves as part of our lives follows the history of the world. In the first world war portable wind-up gramophones were taken to the front so troops could enjoy a little piece of home while on foreign land.

By 1925 electric recording had come in but people still had to carry around cumbersome 78s which could play for a maximum of 4 minutes on each side, though today's record artists would no doubt be amazed to realise that it was usual to record four sides in a single 3 hour session. As records developed so playing times increased.

One interesting development that took place in the 1920s was the picture disc. Drawings on paper were covered with a thin, invisible foil into which grooves were pressed. Originally they displayed pictures of stars of the silent movies along with their greetings and were called Talk 'O' Photos. The idea being patented in 1928 by the French Decca company. Other picture disc developments included a bendable, non-flammable record made of plastic and decorated with writing and small drawings produced by the Goodson company of England. Picture discs including photos came in the 1930s. Advertisers were quick to jump on the bandwagon using the idea to promote their products with pictures and sound. Though these were produced in their thousands they are still sought after by real collectors and can be quite valuable if in good condition.

The same cannot be said of many of the 78s from these early days, however. Newer techniques have come along which make it possible to take away the background noises and distortions from old recordings though even they cannot restore a damaged record. As far back as the thirties the giant RCA company in America was 'cleaning up' its own recordings and now, with compact discs giving brilliant sound, the process is being repeated by record companies around the world devaluing those old scratchy 78s.

During the second world war millions of records were destroyed in a salvage operation which was aimed at reclaiming Shelac, a basic ingredient in those early records. The idea was to turn out new records aimed at boosting moral and the army even went so far as to allow soldiers the chance to record letters to their folks back home. Again these sort of 'oddities' can be valued highly by specialised collectors but the more everyday recordings by people like Gracie Fields, Vera Lynn and Glenn Miller are generally of little or no interest.

Scratches started to disappear from records when Columbia invented the 33 rpm long player using a new material, vinylite, in 1948. Its big rival RCA preferred the 45 rpm single. Both were to survive for years and ensure the boom in record sales that has taken place since the fifties.

The first LPs went on sale in this country in 1949 and some of those early examples are worth money for their curiosity value. So, too are a few of the very early 45s.

In your hideaways you may well have hundreds of

78s. Those from pre-fifties are of little or no value. If they are truly unusual enough to warrant the interest of museums or collectors, you may get a few pounds for them but that is rare indeed. The few exceptions worth noting include:

- advertising discs – like those for Dewars whisky or Standard motor cars
- picture effect records, those featuring music hall acts
- unusual classical performances – generally those by 'unknown' performers
- 'V-Discs' or 'Transcription Discs' which were used either for the armed forces or for radio transmission
- certain obscure jazz and blues artists.

If you own or come across records that fall into these areas then you are probably best off contacting Vintage Record Mart.

Most 78s you are likely to find, however, will date from the early fifties – Perry Como, Guy Mitchell, Frankie Laine and the like – and they are of no value. People seem to think because it's a 78 it must be worth money. It's not, again because modern technology means recordings can be 'cleaned up' and few people are interested in these, frequently heavily distorted, recordings.

Rock and roll records in 78 format can be worth a few pounds, possibly even as much as £10 each, especially those by Elvis Presley and Cliff Richard. In fact it is interesting that Cliff's records up to 1962 were released on 78s as well as 45s. The old style format being used for export, Cliff having a massive following in his native India. That makes them more valuable since most recordings were on 45s by the late fifties. Such a find could be worth as much as £20.

Before we go into more detail about singles, though, let us touch on LPs. It is very difficult to generalise about the 12 inch album. Thousands of millions of

'Here is Elvis Great LP Catalog on RCA Records'.
Source: Topham Library.

these have been made all over the world during the past three decades or more. Certain titles may be of interest to collectors but they would need to be with the original sleeve and in very good condition. In particular there is a market for obscure 1960s and '70s British and American psychedelic and beat groups. These bands – like Kaleidoscope, July, Elias Hulk, Tudor Lodge, Spring, Koobas and Dr Z, to name but a few – would nowadays be classed as 'unknown' amongst the general record buying public but their albums can fetch in excess of £50 in top condition.

There is little point in even suggesting that the average LP is worth anything. Most Beatles long players, for instance, were usually produced in hundreds of thousands, if not in millions, so there are just too many for them to be valuable. An exception would be the Please Please Me album which was first issued on the old style Parlophone label featuring gold writing on black. The mono version of this is worth about £100 and should you come across an original stereo pressing then a collector would be willing to pay at least £400 for your find.

However, as far as LPs generally are concerned it is unusual recordings that are likely to be worth the most money. So if anything you find is non-chart material it is worth checking out with an expert.

Much the same goes for the old 10 inch long playing records. People often think because they are rarely made these days they will be worth money. This is just not the case. One exception is rock and roll. It does not matter whether it is album, extended play singles or the singles themselves. There's a big market for all early material of this kind.

Country and Western music is less popular in this country and for that reason is not as highly valued. However, Hank Williams long players can fetch up to £20 and so do those by some of his contemporaries.

Some of the early country and western style music is really what is called 'hillbilly' which was the forerunner of 'rockabilly'. Rock and roll afficianados are particularly keen on this type of music and that adds to its value.

A couple of times already I've mentioned EPs – extended play singles. These are not so popular now but were very much part of the record scene when 45s were first popular. Often they featured all four tracks from two hit singles by one artist. Very few of these were sold at the time of issue so they are seldom seen these days making them very marketable and well worth trying to sell. Again, though, you will need to have the original cover and the condition will be important.

There are a lot of popular misconceptions about singles and their value. I pointed out earlier that long playing records by popular artists were, in many cases, produced in their thousands and so were the singles. So if the ones you have are all very popular titles you can forget about them having a high value.

There are exceptions, but very few. Where a record was first released on one label and then switched to another before it became a hit then the original version can be worth money. So, too, are the older singles issued with picture covers, as long as they are still together, and unusual imported copies.

You will also find that collectors are keen to acquire singles on the original London and Tamla Motown labels. For example, Billy Eckstine on Tamla Motown is a genuine find.

If any of the singles you discover have 'Demonstration Copy' stamped on them, or 'Not for sale' then that could add to the value. If you are really lucky you might get up to £2 for a pristine copy of one of the first few Beatles singles if it is a regular issue. However, a demo version commands in excess of £150.

90

Having the original paper sleeves the records were sold in adds to the value for a collector. Don't worry if the sleeve is the wrong one or there is no sleeve at all. So long as the record has not been damaged you'll still get a fair price.

Don't expect collectors to pay extra because the records you have all feature one artist and cover his or her whole career. Many people were fans of a particular artist or group and so it is not unusual to find a store that includes many records by one person. It doesn't add to their value though you may well find that one or two of the records included are worth extra because they were not so popular and therefore fewer copies were sold.

For those who are now approaching 'The Golden Years' – middle age – it is difficult to realise just how long ago some fads in music were popular. It is now more than 10 years, for instance, since the punk phenomenon arrived on the music scene. Some of those records are now worth a lot of money to collectors. So if someone in your family had a past when safety pins were used for more than emergency repairs, then it is certainly worth hunting out any records they may have collected.

Should you find among them a copy of the Sex Pistols' God Save The Queen on the A & M label treat it with great respect. Depending on condition it could fetch £300 or more, but don't get excited if your copies are on the Virgin label – there are too many of these to make them of any great value.

It is always important to check the sleeves of records if they are still with them. In the sixties picture covers for 45s were first introduced – though there are a few rare examples from the fifties – and some of these help to make the records worth money even though the records themselves were produced in vast quantities. That includes especially those featuring David Bowie

Beatlemania Hits Sotheby's. Miss Hazel McOmrie holds signed records of the Beatles' first successes, Love Me Do and Please, Please Me. Auctioned on March 3, 1980.
Source: Topham Library.

92

or T Rex and some of the picture sleeved records issued in the seventies.

If you know anything about the early days of artists then it is worth watching out for any of these recordings. For example:

- David Bowie recorded as David Jones and the King Bees or David Jones and the Lower Third on the Vocalian label. There are not too many of those around so watch out for them.

- The Who once recorded as High Numbers a record called Zoot Suit backed with I'm The Face. That is a definite collectors' item.

- If the artist's name is Listen then what you have is an early recording by Robert Plant of the Led Zepplin group – on the Parlophone label – and you could sell it for £100 or more.

- You'll also get that much for a record called Traffic Jam by the Spectres. It is really Status Quo.

What makes these records valuable is the small number that were produced. There arc other examples from the seventies so it is always worth checking out when the group or artist is not listed in any of the books that include details of chart singles. In some cases the first recordings were on private labels with very few being made and those only for promotion.

Talking about promotions there is a whole market for those give-aways from the sixties and seventies. What I'm talking about are the flimsie records, generally called 'flexies', which were often stuck to the outside of magazines or given away as adverts.

Every year, for example, the Beatles fan club sent out one of these flexi-discs free to members. Now they will fetch £40. A much earlier example of a promotion record is Elvis and The Truth About Me. It was on a five inch 78 and was a special offer with Weekend Mail. It cost 2s 1d – about 10.5 new pence. Now it will fetch £40 to £50.

Other special records to look out for include a set of story discs based on the television characters created by Gerry Anderson. These feature series like Thunderbirds and more than 30 different ones were released. Some of these will be worth at least £15 to a collector.

Should you come across a Tamla Motown recording of speeches made by American civil rights campaigner Martin Luther King then it is a true 'find' fetching around £100 if in mint condition.

Do's and Don'ts

- Under no circumstances send records through the post for an initial valuation. Photostat the label and a sleeve if it has one, or take a photograph and send that. Many early records have been re-released on 'look alike' labels. A reputable collectors' shop will want to make certain yours is a true original.

- Beware of going to markets and second-hand stalls. They are unlikely to know the true value and even if they do won't usually give you the same sort of money you'd get from a collector.

- Remember the price you'll get from a collectors' shop is about half of what you'll get by selling it direct to the collector themselves. However, if you go to a reputable dealers they are likely to have a list of regular customers who are looking for particular records and willing to pay a good price. In that case you could benefit as well.

- A number of magazines are published for record collectors. It is worth buying one and checking out the adverts. You will soon discover the shops that will be interested in your records and will give you a fair price.

- Only sell to a dealer who will pay you an agreed price straight away. Do not give the records to a dealer to sell for you. The system is open to a lot of abuse and there are many poor people who have gone back to find the shop has closed down or there is a different and unhelpful face behind the counter!

- Magazines will also include adverts from individual collectors who want to obtain particular records. You may be lucky to find one looking for what you have to sell. Alternatively you might like to advertise the records you've discovered. However, remember a good dealer will take the difficulty out of finding a buyer and save you the cost of advertising. At least you'll end up with something in your pocket.

- Never be intimidated into selling. If you are not sure you're being offered a fair price, phone other dealers and get them to quote first. No single book will give you a complete run-down on records and their values. The only ones ever produced are now way out of date and totally unreliable as far as a guide to current prices is concerned.

Summary

– Old 78s are not usually worth anything. Nor are mass produced singles and albums. There were just too many of them to make them valuable.

– Special sleeves, extra printing on the label – like Demo copies – and any 'unusual' features may add to the value.

– Early, less popular recordings by well known artists are often worth more than their hit singles.

– The condition is important and an original sleeve will often add to the value.

– Rock and Roll records are collectors items though not as valuable as some more specialist discs.

– Look at collector's magazines or go to reputable specialist shops if the records are valuable and you want a guide to what they are worth.

Contacts

If you cannot find a specialist shop in your area or need some expert guidance, Beanos, 27 Surrey Street, Croydon CR0 1RR are willing to help, but you MUST enclose a stamped, addressed envelope.

Following some articles in the *Daily Mirror* recently they had to take on extra staff to cope with the flood of mail. Only around 10 per cent of the enquiries related to records that were of real value so although the shop's boss, David Lashmar says he is happy to help anyone who thinks the records they've discovered may be of value, he does need the SAE to ensure a reply.

CHAPTER EIGHT:
SILVER

Something quite remarkable has happened to the price of silver during the past twenty years. For two decades after the end of the Second World War the price had held steadily at just under 10s an ounce – 50p in today's money. Then it suddenly doubled almost overnight, doubled again in a matter of five years or so and has since leapt again. Today it is around £3.60 an ounce.

That means any genuine silver item you may find hidden away has an automatic minimum value. You can always sell it as scrap. Indeed that was the way silver pieces used to be valued even in auction houses. The auctioneer's clerk would be armed with a ready reckoner – no modern calculators were available then. An old auction catalogue shows us what that meant: 'A silver coffee-pot with a moulded dome cover, foliage and strapwork by Paul de Lamerie, London hallmark 1728 – 25 ounces at 150 shillings per ounce.' So the particular piece in question would have fetched £187 10s which, according to one of the experts at Christie's, was roughly equal to what a labourer would have earned in a year. Compare that with a George II coffee pot by Lamerie dated 1749 which was sold at Christie's, New York, in 1986 for the equivalent of £35,500.

Everybody knows, of course, that it is easy to spot whether something is really made of silver because of

A Continental model of a grouse with hinged wings and detachable head, Berthold Muller 10½ inches, 26.7503. Sold 15 August 1988 for £572, and a Continental model of a Maribou Stork, 10¾ inches. Sold 15 August for £440.
Source: Christie's.

the hallmark. It will also tell you the year a piece was made and where, since different cities have different hallmarks. However, it is not quite as easy as it sounds. Small items of English silver have not always been hallmarked and sometimes the hallmark will wear off with age. Worse still, fake hallmarks have been added on occasions so there is no absolute guarantee one way or the other. Obviously knowing something about hallmarks will help you identify your find. Usually there are four punch-marks: the makers, the assay office, the quality and the date letter. The sovereign's head was usually included on silver between 1784 and 1890 and King George and Queen Mary commemorated their Silver Jubilee by having their heads stamped on silver between 1933 and 1936. There are a number of books on hallmarks and you should find that your local library stocks at least one of them.

Out and out fakes cannot be sold legally in this country and any reputable dealer will tell you this. If someone claims an item is fake and then offers to buy it from you do not accept. Go instead to another dealer or an auction house and find out the truth. Either it is genuine in which case probably worth much more than you were being offered or it is a fake and you would have been breaking the law to sell it. However, if it is a genuine piece of silver that you discover, in addition to the guarantee of at least scrap value, you may well have a rewarding find. As in the case of the Lamerie coffee pot the price it will fetch is often only loosely connected to the underlying value of the silver. A rare George IV Irish dog collar with the crest of a celebrated actor date 1828 and weighing less than two ounces was sold at Christie's in 1985 for £700.

Silver also has the advantage that it doesn't crack as often as china nor does it chip, come unstuck or generally deteriorate. Even if it gets dented it can usually be returned to its former glory relatively simply. Just don't try and do it yourself. You could damage the design or mar the piece in such a way as to drastically reduce its value. Talking of damaging the value, Christie's came up with an interesting piece a couple of years ago. Originally it had been a pair of wine-coasters made in London in 1789 by a silversmith PPP. They would have been worth up to £800 had they been left as they were. However, some misguided owner had tired of the coasters and persuaded a silversmith to refashion them into a sugar basket by adding feet, base and a swing handle. In that form it cannot be legally sold though Christie's believe it could be returned to its former glory and turned again into something worth selling.

Teasets, trays and salvers are currently selling for up to £16 an ounce though the price will reflect the quality and attractiveness of the pieces. Flatware – plates, saucers and cutlery – is generally valued slightly lower at up to £13 an ounce, though complete sets of cutlery made by the same maker and hallmarked in the same year can fetch consideraly more. In this case you can reckon on at least £20 an ounce. More delicate items like cake or fruit bowls, sweet dishes and baskets of all kinds often sell for more than £20 an ounce. However, it is important to differentiate between silver and fused plate where a thin silver skin covered a much thicker layer of copper. The latter will clearly not be valued on a total weight basis.

Over the years silver has been used as a means to pay off soldiers and a way to cash in on one's fortune when times got hard. During Britain's Civil War a lot of silver was melted down for cash and so many older items were lost. However, it is still possible to find ancient candle holders and if you should make such a find you can be on a real winner. In fact, you are more likely to find candlesticks made since the middle of the last century. Many are weighted with other metals so you must expect the price to reflect this. It is also true that old candlesticks are sometimes re-cast. Provided that the end product is again submitted to assay that is no problem, but if it hasn't been then again you cannot legally sell.

Candlesticks are often sold – and found – in pairs. If the hallmarks on both tally, then together they can be worth considerably more than if sold separately. However, some quirk of our forefathers seems to have led to a 'mix and match' philosophy and all too frequently the hallmarks do not tally. If that turns out to be the case be prepared to accept a lower price. A pair of matching Victorian candlesticks dating from 1875 were sold at Christie's in 1986 for £480 and certainly you should expect to get more than £300 for a reasonable pair.

As silver has always been regarded as decorative as well as functional you may well find items like buckles and buttons made of silver. A lot of 12 silver buttons was auctioned for £85 in 1986 at the same time as a pair of Art Nouveau buckles were sold for £40. Hair combs, slides, grips and hat pins can also be found in silver as well as posy holders. All are worth checking out with silversmiths, reliable jewellers or an auction house. You may also find that silver has been used in connection with other items as either decoration or as lids, mounts or feet.

Silver has also been used over the years for models and sculptures. There are many examples from as far back as the sixteenth and seventeenth centuries. Though age may have a bearing on price the main judgement will be made on craftsmanship. This was well reflected in a sale at Christie's in 1986 when two silver cream jugs were on offer. One, in the shape of a goat, was made in London in 1840 and showed high quality and good workmanship. It produced a bid of

A pair of George III candlesticks, James Waterhouse and Co., Sheffield 1774, 12½ inches high. Sold 15 August 1988 for £2,090.
Source: Christie's.

£2,000. The other, a dog in more senses than one was of unmarked Continental silver and went for only £280. Even silver, though, is only saleable when there is a buyer. A pair of new Italian model pheasants which were offered for sale in 1986 failed to find a buyer at £70. According to the experts they lacked quality and substance. A year earlier a crododile made in Birmingham in 1914 which weighed only 33 ounces but which was finely chased went for a remakable £2,100.

As designs and styles of silver products vary so tremendously there is not a great deal – other than the basic hallmark – that can be gleaned from books and

A Victorian shaped circular cake stand, John Frazer and Edward Haws, London 1981, 8 inches, 27.2503. Sold 13 Septefmber for £528.
Source: Christie's.

you really do need to take this sort of find to someone who can give you a true valuation. According to the experts, however, many of the items taken to them for valuation are, in fact, electro-plated nickel silver (EPNS). If they date from the beginning of this century, then instead of a hallmark they will have the EPNS initials on them. However, there was no such mark before that so again this is not a hard and fast rule and the object will need valuing by an expert. It could be worth your while to do so. Five years ago people used to turn their noses up if something was EPNS but times have changed. Now, particularly for items made before the turn of the century, good prices are being paid.

Obviously the more intricate the work the better the price. A pretty Victorian tea and coffee set – the tea and coffee pot plus sugar bowl and cream jug – could be worth as much as £500. Particular makers are of interest as well. Although Dr Christopher Dresser was a Victorian designer his style is very similar to Art Deco: stark and angular. Recently a plated toast rack designed by the good doctor went for £10,000 at auction. Size is important as far as EPNS is concerned as well. While a teaspoon may be worth no more than 10p, a soup ladle might fetch £10.

Dos and Don'ts

- Don't try to hammer out any dents on silverware yourself.
- Do look for a hallmark.
- Don't assume it is not silver just because you cannot find the hallmark. It may have worn off or be hidden from view.
- Do take silver items to reputable dealers and always seek two or three valuations. Or go to an auction house.

CHAPTER NINE:
STAMPS

Stamp collecting is one of the world's most popular hobbies. It has interested children of both sexes and all ages for more than 100 years with many collections starting off as nothing more than a hotch potch group of scruffy stamps stuck in a book bought at Woolworths. More frequently than not such stamp collections just sort of grow – rather like Topsy. Auction houses reckon they look at two or three hundred collections a week and if you multiply this by the many hundreds of stamp dealers around the country it is clear to see just how many collections there are tucked away. Most, say the experts are not worth anything and their suggestion is to pass the collection on to a youngster. Even so they are anxious not to pass up the opportunity to examine any find you might make following an amazing incident a couple of years ago when Richard Ashton of Sotheby's was looking at collections brought to the auctioneers' Copenhagen headquarters. Many were well presented, smartly laid out but of little real value. Then a man walked in with an old exercise book which, says Ashton, is not unusual. Not expecting the contents to be of much interest the stamp expert glanced through the 100 or so stamps included in the book. Suddenly to his surprise his eye latched on to one specimen that he just could not believe was tucked away in such a mundane collection. Cut from bluish paper it was

Franked postcard with one penny stamp.

printed with a red crowned circle inside which were the words: Paid at Hamilton, Bermuda. It was issued by William Perot, Postmaster of Hamilton and was not so much a stamp as a sort of postmark. When it was sold at auction it fetched £36,300 and yet the man who had brought the collection to Ashton had bought it from the widow of a Danish sailor and had owned it for nearly ten years without knowing he had anything of value.

All stamp experts are anxious to point out that such finds are the exception rather than the rule though it clearly pays to get a professional valuation rather than just discard the collection because it appears haphazard and slipshod. However, there are ways to judge whether a collection you unearth is likely to be of value. Before we discuss that, lets look at the origins of stamps.

Britain's first postmaster was Thomas Withering who was appointed in 1632 but, like his modern counterpart, he had to face a barrage of complaints about delays. His answer was to introduce the first postmarks to show the date of 'posting'. At that time there were mail services of sorts throughout Europe, but it took another 200 years for the idea of a properly regulated postal system with stamps to be introduced and even then it met with opposition from people with vested interests in leaving the system as it was.

Rowland Hill was the pioneer of the Penny Post. Originally a schoolmaster, he went to work as a secretary to the South Australian Commissioners. In 1837 he put forward his scheme for an overall 1d postage charge for letters but hit opposition from Lord Lichfield, the then Postmaster General, his secretary Col. William Maberly and the Duke of Wellington, a powerful figure in parliament. These three believed Hill's plans would destroy priveleges they held in the old mail coach and postboy system. Anyone who claims today's post charges are too high need only look back and see what Lichfield and his friends were trying to safeguard in the nineteenth century. A single sheet letter sent from London to Edinburgh would have cost 1½d (6p). Two sheets would have doubled the cost and if the letter weighed an ounce it was charged as if it was four sheets. So what would cost you no more than 19p now would have cost the equivalent of 22½p then! Eventually, however, Hill's proposals were accepted by the government and he was appointed to a position at the treasury. Parliament passed the Uniform Penny Postage Act in 1839 and it came into force on January 10, 1840. Letters were carried to destinations throughout England, Scotland, Wales and Ireland for 1d per half ounce paid in advance – there were still no stamps at that time.

It was not long before artists and engravers were set to work on the idea of a stamp to note that the letter had been pre-paid. At the same time William Mulready was commissioned to design envelopes and wrappers. These first saw the light of day on May 1 1840 and were available for public use on May 6. They

107

*House of Commons special postage arrangements plus
assortment of ½d, one penny and two pence stamps.*

showed Britannia sending out winged messengers to the four points of the compass – and introduced the first postage 'error' since one of the angels appeared to have only one leg! However, the public didn't like them and the press blasted the idea, though if you've one today it is worth money. At least £50 and possibly as much as £1,000.

During those early months of 1840 members of the Houses of Parliament were given a special privelege of free franking and then a special envelope which also cost nothing. It's reckoned that many members massively abused the system but that has not stopped such letters becoming scarce and if you think you have one of these you must get it valued. It's unlikely to be worth less than £300. Probably because Mulready's envelope was so badly received by the general public it came in for some Victorian satire. There were comic versions issued, one showing a hanged postman. Bids for such an item today would be likely to start at around £1,000. These envelopes were rejected by the public in favour of the little label stamps with 'glutinous wash' on the backs. In the margin between the stamps was this advisory message: 'In wetting the Back be careful not to remove cement.'

The world's first adhesive stamps were the Penny Black and the Two Pence Blue issued in Britain in 1840 and only on sale for a year. They did not include any words to indicate the country of origin, just Victoria's head. To this very day the monarch's head is reckoned sufficient to indicate a British stamp. One of the great myths about stamps is the huge values people seem to think are attached to Penny Blacks. Very recently a record £65,000 was paid at a London auction house for one but the value depends on the condition, the heaviness of the postmark and whether it has a border on all four sides. Since the stamps were issued in large sheets without perforations they had to be cut and if the scissors slipped and part of the design is missing then your stamp is certainly not worth thousands or even hundreds of pounds. In fact, a used Penny Black that was badly cut from the sheet might be worth no more than a fiver. The Two Pence Blue is a rarer stamp so even damaged can be worth £30 or more. Should you discover either kind in unused, mint condition then you're onto a real winner. The value could be ten times the price for a used stamp!

If these, or any stamps you find, are attached to envelopes then do not try to separate them. Family correspondence from the nineteenth century is often worth a great deal of money and the envelope and postmark with the stamp attached will be worth more than the envelope and stamp separately. In fact, many collectors are more interested in postal history these days than in just stamps.

If evidence was needed of the success of Rowland Hill's idea then it came quickly. In 1839 a total of 76 million letters were sent pre-paid. In 1840, 169 million letters were sent and within five years the figure had doubled. Strange as it may seem that was still not enough to convince people abroad of the value of the British system. They felt that you had to pay when you received a letter or else it wouldn't be delivered. The Swiss Cantons – before the Confederation – were among the first to follow Britain's lead and issue adhesive stamps. Zurich stamps came first in March 1843 and then Geneva produced a curiosity, a divisible stamp, in October of the same year.

Brazil was the first large country to follow the lead when they issued the so-called Bulls-eye stamps on August 1, 1843. Then, in 1845 the Canton of Basle produced its first issue featuring doves. The postmaster of New York issued his own stamps in the same year and in April 1847 a stamp was issued by the captain of a steamship which carried mail locally round the coast of Trinidad. That was also the year when Mauritius became the first British colony to issue stamps and when the first US government stamps were produced. Bermuda followed in 1848, Belgium and France in 1849 and over the next fifteen years most of Europe, the States and British possessions joined in.

Collecting stamps began almost as soon as the stamps were issued. In Christmas 1861 a booklet was printed in Paris: Catalogue des Timbres-Poste crees dans les divers Etats du Globe. It was compiled by Alfred Potiquet and listed 1,080 adhesive stamps and 132 stamped envelopes. A second edition appeared in March 1862 which listed 1,253 items and rival catalogues appeared in Paris, Brussels and England where Frederick Booty published Aids to Stamp Collectors in Brighton in April 1862. Today's catalogues are huge tomes in comparison with Britain alone issuing several 'special' sets of stamps a year now. The most widely used is the one produced by Stanley Gibbons who are acknowledged stamp experts. However, the prices quoted in their catalogue are only rough guides as far as trying to sell stamps is concerned. You would be lucky in most cases for a dealer to offer you more than a third of the Gibbons price.

Auction houses are interested in stamps of high values but, while they will give you a guide as to values they will not buy small value examples from you or even, in most cases arrange for a sale. So you will have to go to a dealer to sell most of the stamps you find. Condition is also important. If the stamps have been stuck down in a book then they have probably lost most of their value. Even if the famed stamp hinges were used you could see the value halved. Whatever condition the stamps are in when you find them leave them as they are. Any further 'playing' with them may damage them to the point where they are totally

Selection of stamps including £1 Postal Union Congress London 1929.

worthless.

Prices of stamps today are beginning to pick up after a disastrous collapse in the market in 1980. Prior to this many people had been encouraged to invest their hard earned savings in postage stamps and many fortunes were lost. You may be lucky enough for a close relative to have been tempted in this way and then just tucked their collection away when the bottom fell out of the market. To show what the collapse meant in money terms it is worth looking at the Postal Union Congress £1 Black stamp which shows St. George slaying the dragon. In 1965 that would have been worth £8, by 1975 it was fetching £35 but by 1979 when the stamp world had gone investment crazy the price had risen to £1,600. Today in good condition one is likely to be sold for £300 at the most. Nonetheless a good increase on the price twenty years ago.

Most collections you are likely to unearth in the attic will be the schoolboy type but just may contain one of those 'diamonds' that are occasionally to be found in coalmines. According to one expert the most common, but valuable stamp in these sort of collections is a George V Silver Jubilee stamp. In good condition one might fetch a couple of hundred pounds. The real gems, however, are the 'freak' stamps, those with printing errors. As far as anyone knows there is only one example of the 1867 Virgin Islands stamp which does not have the picture of the Virgin on it. However, if you know different . . . another example could be worth well over £20,000. A similar price could be expected if you discovered one of the 1918 United States 24 cent stamps on which a picture of a plane was printed upside down.

Judging a Collection

Here is a list of twelve points to help you judge whether a collection you've unearthed is a valuable

113

find or more likely to be a nice gift for your children or grandchildren.

(1) Is there any record of steady spending on the collection particularly on unusual stamps? Look out for several consecutive new issues.

(2) Are there receipts to show stamps have been bought from auctioneers or specialist dealers?

(3) Is there any evidence the collection has ever been insured?

(4) Has the collection ever been professionally valued before?

(5) Has the collection ever been professionally exhibited – there may be diplomas, certificates of participation or even medals?

(6) If the album is in an old exercise book or a standard stamp collecting book like those sold by Woolworths – Black Cat is the best known – then it is unlikely to be of real value.

(7) It is likely to contain at least some gems if the album is one of the following: Lallier, Oppers, Imperial, Ideal, Godden, Stanley Gibbons, Oriel, GMS Blue or Philatelic.

(8) Does the collection include stamps accompanied by certificates of genuineness from expert committees like the Royal Philatelists Society or the British Philatelists Association?

(9) Does the album include just the stamps of one country? This shows a set pattern and may well indicate a higher quality collection.

(10) Does the collection contain mint condition stamps up to £1 face value or its foreign equivalent from more than 20 years ago?

(11) Does the collection consist in the main of mint stamps in sets including the high denomination

ones as well as the low?

(12) Does the collection consist of, or include a substantial section of postal history with stamps still attached to envelopes?

Says one expert: "If in answering the questions people find there are positive points to the album then it could well turn out to be of value. As we've seen you never can tell, even some others – like the one which turned up in Copenhagen – may include something of value and are worth having professionally valued."

"The only collections which in all probability are going to have virtually no value are: childhood collections made up of stamps soaked off envelopes – the most common finds – or of mint low face value stamps from packets, something else we see a lot of; collections consisting of modern issues or first day covers," say the experts. It is reckoned that of every 20 stamp collections an auctioneer inspects 18 or 19 are childhood collections of little value, but most reputable auctioneers are happy to check to make sure for owners without making a charge.

Do's and Dont's

• Do show the ENTIRE collection to a reputable auctioneer or dealer. He can only examine what you show him, so if you want the collection valued show him all of it. Unless the collection is highly specialised it can be examined in your presence and a fairly accurate indication of its value given on the spot.

• Do make an appointment with the expert. Most reputable auctioneers and dealers make no charge for a verbal valuation but the numbers of professional stamp experts, those who can value almost any philatelic collections put in front of them, is surprisingly small – fewer than 20 even in London. So the expertise is in demand and their time is valuable. However, most do travel around the country and you may find a local 'open day' when you are encouraged to bring along collections.

- Don't handle the stamps.
- Don't hinge them to album pages – a tip worth passing on to children if they are starting a collection.
- Don't soak stamps off envelopes. They may be 20, 200, 2,000 or even 20,000 times more valuable on the envelope.
- Don't spend hours making lists of stamps or hours adding up all the 'prices' in stamp catalogues. An expert values the stamp by looking at the actual stamps and not by looking at lists of them. This is because the composition of a collection is more easily determined by an examination of the stamps themselves and because condition is all important.
- Don't let anyone pick from the collection before it has been examined by a professional stamp expert.
- Don't be surprised by the time, or lack of it, that an expert takes to value a collection. If an expert is regularly looking at 200 to 300 albums a week it would normally be possible for him to value an album fairly accurately within five or ten minutes. His first look will tell him quite a deal about who formed it. Occasionally even the smell of the album may provide some clues.

Contacts

- Stanley Gibbons, 399 Strand, London WC2 are the country's best known dealers.
- Auction houses usually have experts who can value collections.
- There are many regular publications on stamp collecting and stamp values.

CHAPTER TEN:
TOYS

As long as there have been children there have been toys – playthings to keep the young monsters amused while their parents get on with the day-to-day chores. Dolls in various forms, made of everything from bronze to wood, are the chief examples that have survived since early times. However, there are also examples of bronze and pottery animals plus ivory and silver beasts from India and the Far East.

Medieval European toys were made of carved and painted wood or leather stuffed with hair or chopped straw. Children will always be children and toys have born the brunt of their over-enthusiasm. For that reason there are few examples remaining in tact of very early toys. The chances of you finding one in your attic is indeed remote!

Nurembourg, still regarded as the home of lead soldiers, was the centre for earliest commercial production in late-medieval times but, again, few examples have survived. However, the toys of the rich from the late seventeenth century through to the nineteenth, can still be found and are highly treasured. Originally these were produced as trinkets and trifles for adults but the well-off frequently let their children play with them. They were usually made in expensive materials such as silver or porcelain but they can also be found in brass or pottery.

Early British rocking horses dating from the

seventeenth century looked more like boats than horses, with the horse's legs painted on side pieces. Other early toys included roller-skates, jack-in-the-boxes, yo-yos and bows and arrows. The earliest jigsaws, dating from the mid-eighteenth century, were mounted and boxed in mahogany and were made by Wallis and Son, the map makers. So, not surprisingly, they depicted maps.

In the nineteenth century there were Sunday toys, including picture blocks of religious subjects and educational card games based on the Happy Families idea. This was also the time when Bavarian toymakers started producing more mechanical toys. Early examples of clockwork or electric working models of locomotives and toy trains, complete with rolling stock, made by companies like Marklin and Bing, are now highly prized. A Marklin gauge 1 GNR teak-finished passenger coach was sold for £260 in 1985 at the same time as a quantity of rolling stock by Bing was auctioned for £480. A year later a carriage from the Kaiser Train made by Bing around 1901 sold for £770. Anything from this set can be identified by a crown under the window.

Some mechanical toys like those made by scientific instrument makers Bassett-Lowke, were so detailed that they could hardly be regarded as playthings. One of their British Railways Class 5 locomotives was sold for £1,100 in 1986 and a Flying Scotsman went for £700 in 1986, £150 more than a similar model had fetched just over a year earlier.

At the cheaper end of the market Bavaria and Saxony were the homes for early tinplate toys which ranged from penny whistles to hollow, die-stamped pop guns and pistols, and from clowns to performing animals. These were generally on sale from the middle of the nineteenth century until the outbreak of the second world war. Often referred to as 'penny' toys –

though even at the turn of the century they would have cost more than that – these usually measure about three and a half inches and show very little detail. Such examples as early buses, aeroplanes and fire engines are of interest but unlikely to fetch much more than a few pounds. However, if you do come across examples showing more detail then your find could be worth a few hundred pounds. Those made in Nuremburg seem particularly popular, especially if they have the name Lehmann – a four-seater open tourer from this manufacturer fetched £600 a couple of years ago. These toys are not valuable if broken but should you have the original box as well as a complete toy then its value will be higher. A Lehmann baker and sweep with its box made around 1905 was sold for £1,600 in 1985 and £2,700 in September 1988. It measured five and a quarter inches. A more common Lehmann toy, the beetle, was produced in vast quantities for thirty years. Even so one in good condition could fetch £100.

French tinplate toys are also worth money. A small airship made by Tipp, even though it was missing several parts, reached £250 at auction in 1985. Even more modern tinplate toys will fetch good money including the Chad Valley examples from the 1930s and Schuco clockwork toys which were made between the 1930s and the 1950s. However, the Japanese toys of the 50s and 60s need to be in mint condition with their boxes to be worth anything notable and even then you'll be unlikely to get more than £25. Hornby trains are popular, an early pre-war LNER locomotive was sold at Christie's for £190 in 1986.

Even cheaper than the tinplate toys were the so-called wooden Bristol toys which were made in cottages and small back street sweat shops. Although they originated in Bristol they were also made in Birmingham, London and other industrial cities. Model coaches, Noah's arks and farms with primitive

121

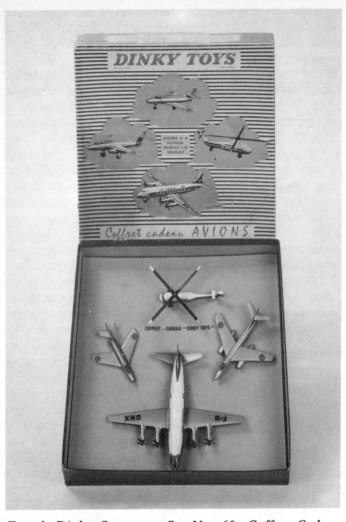

French Dinky Supertoys Set No. 60, Coffret Cadeau Avions, including Mystere IVa, Vantgour, Sikorsky S.58 and a Viscount Air Liner in original box. Sold 22 September 1988 for £275.
Source: Christie's.

animals were also made out of wood in Britain and Germany. In 1985 Christie's sold a German Noah's Ark with 75 pairs of animals and people dating from around 1880 for £650.

Since World War II tinplate has been replaced by metal castings made with the highest precision and attention to detail especially for the production of miniature cars. Cast metal is still being used today despite the preponderance of plastic. Best known cast metal playthings are Dinky Toys, the first being made in 1933 by Frank Hornby who was also responsible for the trains and Meccano. By the way if you find any Meccano it is not valuable if rusted or worn and the 'bits and pieces' can only be sold on market stalls. However in sets, in original boxes and with instructions Meccano can be worth several hundred pounds.

The first Dinky toys were a tank, two sports cars, a tractor, a motor truck and a delivery van cast in heavy lead alloy with metal wheels. Two early vans went for £400 and £420 respectively at auction in 1986 and two sports cars fetched £320 and £380 each. White rubber tyres and tinplate radiators as well as the addition of chassis to some models had been introduced by World War II. There was also a much more comprehensive range which included vans and army vehicles, ships, aeroplanes, trams and buses, farm animals and road signs. Limited production continued during the war with full production returning in April 1946. A range of Supertoys was introduced in 1948. One of these, a blue Guy van advertising Ever Ready in mint condition but without its box was sold for £60 in 1985.

It's not just Dinky Toys that are in demand. A first series of Matchbox models went for £160 in 1986 and in the previous year a mint condition set of the six Models of Yesteryear, introduced in 1956, sold for £95 even though they were unboxed. Corgi toys from the

Model of a butcher's shop, circa 1850, made for G. F. Peck (Family Butcher) London E2. Sold for £4,840. Source: Christie's.

1960s can be valuable if in their original boxes – a collection of 25 in mint condition were sold for £400 in 1985. Collectors are also keen on other makers like Rio, Teckno and Spot On.

Toys often reflect the age in which they were produced matching changes in fashion and developments in the world generally including latest inventions. Rear-Admiral Edward Perry of the United States Navy became the first man to reach the North Pole in 1909. To mark the occasion F. Martin, a French toymaker, produced a charming model called La Conquete du Nord which was intended to be a plaything. An example was sold for £1,430 in March 1987.

Toy banks from America are always in demand. Examples include a bulldog which tosses a coin into the air and catches it in his mouth, a soldier who fires a coin at a pigeon; a footballer who kicks a coin into a goal; and, commonest of all, the 'Jolly Nigger Boy' who lifts the coin to his mouth and swallows it. These were produced between 1870 and 1910 and many carry the names of real American banks although they were exported to Britain in large quantities. A few, like the 'British Lion' were made here. The more common of the these will probably fetch £30 or so with some rarer examples likely to be valued at a few hundred pounds.

Rocking horses of all ages are popular with collectors and so can be quite highly valued. Those from the Victorian period are generally beautifully carved and some were constructed on bow pillar rockers. One like this, which was about four feet long, was sold at Christie's in 1985 for £450. A fairly modern one, just over four feet, went for £350 at the same sale but a repainted horse went for just £100 more recently. Again if you find old rocking horses do not try and restore them yourself – all you will probably succeed in doing is reducing their value.

Model soldiers are always popular and the very earliest examples, particularly those made in southern Germany can be quite valuable. The horses and knights were cast in solid bronze, gilded and enamelled while the soldiers were made of slate. In due course, tin and alloys replaced bronze and slate and by the eighteenth and nineteenth centuries the Nuremberg toymakers had produced sets representing most of the soldiers of Europe as well as civilians and animals. These early examples were flat or two dimensional but those made by Heinrichsen or Heyde can be worth money. Five sets of Heinrichsen Napoleonic painted lead figures in original boxes made around 1880 were sold for £130 in 1986.

It was the French who developed 'rond bosses' or solid figures in the 1870s. Towards the end of the century William Britain made the first hollow-cast three-dimensional figures. These were more realistic than the German ones and cheaper because they contained less metal, so they captured the market. Britain expanded and, by the outbreak of World War II could supply every regiment in the British army. A Britain's army staff car in its original box was sold for £250 in 1985.

Early British models have round bases in place of the Continental square ones and are highly prized, especially in sets and even more so if they are complete with their original box. More specialist items include those made by Roger Benoud and Robert Courtenay of Slough which can sell for up to £100 per model.

Do's and Don'ts

- If you find old toys do treat them with care but don't try to wash them or clean them up in any way. Today's modern cleaning agents can seriously damage the old paints and materials so reducing the value of your 'find'.

- Do look for the original boxes and don't throw away any packaging that you might find with the toys. Also keep any instructions or leaflets that might be with them. All these things can add to the value.

Summary

It is very difficult to generalise about toys but age and condition are important as with many of the things you may find lurking in your private treasure trove. However, even damaged toys can be worth hard cash so do not despair if your find is not in perfect condition.

Obviously the more common a toy the less it is likely to be worth. Although in some cases of old toys which were popular a century ago their rarity value has increased with the years since many may have been broken or destroyed. A good example of how toys can appreciate in value is the Britain's khaki RHA set. In 1984 a set was sold for £6,000, but just a year later another set went for £7,200. The sets are rare because only a few were produced between 1938 and 1940. However, publicity about the prices these two fetched flushed out some more sets which sad to say subsequently sold for less at auctions in London and New York as people realised the sets were not as rare as they had thought.

Dolls

Dolls in one form or another have been with us since the earliest times, but they were not the children's playthings we know today. Evidence that there were early human figures – the word doll was certainly not

127

used that long ago – has been found in every part of the globe. There were the ritual dolls of the Mayas and Incas, the fertility dolls of Africa and the carved wooden figures of Polynesia.

However, children's dolls as we know them are relatively modern dating from the end of the middle ages as far as Europe is concerned. The idea then, as now, was for children, especially young girls, to imitate their mothers and that is why dolls were originally made to look like children. In fact, these playthings were called babies until the late seventeenth century when the word doll first came into use.

This accounts for the fact that early dolls tend to have disproportionately large heads and wide-eyed expressions. Even when the figures were supposed to represent older people – as when they were dressed in traditional costumes – they still tended to have infantile faces.

There is no evidence of commercial production of dolls until the early nineteenth century and most before that time were probably made by parents and relatives. German pegwooden dolls were probably the first to be produced on a commercial basis, in around 1820. Ten years later dolls with wax heads started to appear and these were known as 'slit-heads' because tufts of hair were pushed into a slit in the head. An early example of a slit-head would today be worth around £500 in good condition.

In the 1850s the English wax doll was given an extra refinement by Italian emigree Augusta Montanari and her son Richard Napolean. They hit on the idea of using a hot needle so that each individual strand of hair could be inserted into the doll's head. Montanari dolls are noted for their realistic flesh colours, their short necks and the fact that they have stuffed linen bodies onto which chubby limbs are sewn. One like this, from around 1850, with restored legs was recently

128

sold at auction for £400.

Another Italian emigree whose dolls are now much sought after is Pierrotti. Domenico Pierrotti married an English girl and was naturalised in 1810. Henry was born in this country and followed in his father's doll-making footsteps. Pierrotti dolls were made for 150 years from 1780 onwards. Many are puce-tinted and blue eyed but some have a more ethereal quality and natural look. While it is unlikely you'll unearth one just lying in an attic it would be a real find if you did. A poured wax doll, thought to be by Pierrotti with an unusual small open-closed mouth and short hair inserted in slashes in the scalp was sold for £450 in 1985.

Poured wax dolls are the so-called 'aristocrats' of the wax dolls. The wax was poured directly into the mould and allowed to harden to the thickness of about one eighth of an inch before the residue was tipped out. Delicately painted, with a finishing powder dusted over the cheeks they had glass eyes and hair inserted with a hot needle.

As the dolls were fragile, Victorian children were made to treasure them and this has meant some appearing in auction houses in their original condition and elaborate layers of clothing. Some still have notes to the original owners from loving aunts and grandparents and these, should you find them with the dolls in your attic, add to the value.

One of the few native Englishmen in the reckoning when it comes to really exquisite dolls – and those that fetch very high prices – is Charles Marsh. His Nordic dolls from the late nineteenth century were gloriously crowned with mohair or human hair and are quickly snapped up when they are up for auction. Prices range up to about £500.

The only other British name worth looking out for is Lucy Peck. A poured wax doll with her trade mark

*Bisque headed character doll, 20 inches high, marked
1299. Halbig stuffing. Sold 7 July 1988 for £990.
Source: Christie's.*

stamped on it was sold for £1,320 in 1986. However, it was unusual because the eyes closed by means of a wire through the body.

Doll collectors prefer two types above all others. These are the late nineteenth century German and French bisque bebe dolls. Bisque is a very fine unglazed china with a quite magnificent egg-shell finish. It was perfected in France and Germany between 1865 and the 1930s when the arrival of Hitler on the scene put a stop to many fine things, though that has helped to increase the value of those that remain. Since the bisque is even more fragile than an egg shell they are, however, becoming rarer.

Early examples of bisque dolls from the mid-nineteenth century are mainly German and attached to bodies of either kid or composition wood. Something like this could be worth as much as £1,000. So good – and cheap – were the first German bisque heads that the French factories were reduced to buying them for many years until their own quality and design had caught up with the Germans.

French bisque dolls are very different from their German counterparts. The French ones have wide staring eyes, pert noses, cheeks with perfectly symmetrical dimples and what are frequently described as 'rich, warm lips'. The best are the work of Bru, Jumeau, Jules Nicholas Steiner, Huret and Rohmer. One of the most sought after Jumeau dolls has a long face and closed mouth. A typical example from around 1890 recently sold for a staggering £7,500 at auction. The name of the manufacturer of French dolls from this period was usually impressed on them, more often than not on the base of the neck.

German dolls are reckoned to have more character. This is attributed to the fact that instead of idealising a child's face the German dolls were designed by professional sculptors using children as models.

131

Such dolls have real expressions on their faces. They can be pouting, crying or even smiling. They can look out of the corner of their eyes, may well open their mouths – and even reveal teeth – and have interesting hairstyles. Among the best known makers are Kammer & Reinhardt, Simon & Halbig, J. D. Kestner, Armand Marseille and the Heubach brothers.

After 1875 the Simon & Halbig dolls carried an S & H mark and were even more adventurous than those from rival firms. Many were multi-racial, wore national costumes and sometimes boasted pierced ears and primitive voice boxes. To discover one of these would not only be exciting but also very rewarding. Your find could be worth anything from £200 to £3,000.

French response to these innovations included double faced dolls, walking dolls, and even dolls which appear to breathe. Should your treasure trove produce one of these it could be sold for at least £1,000.

All bisque dolls, often called Candy Store Dolls by collectors, which might have cost no more than two shillings (that's ten new pence) a century ago will fetch between £50 and £100 today. They are pretty, small enough to fit into the palm of your hand and at the turn of the century were sold in corner shops along with the groceries, sweets and other inexpensive toys.

One version, the Kewpie Doll was originally designed by Rose O'Neill who retained the patents but let a number of firms produce the dolls. They are recognized by their impish faces, moulded hair and wigs. Their painted features include large eyes glancing to the side, water melon mouths and chubby bodies. A round label on the back, and a red or gold paper heart or shield on the chest marked one of these special all-bisque dolls. One example sold by Christie's in 1987 went for £160 despite having a broken foot and chipped finger.

Around the turn of the century dolls started to improve in quality and definition. As they increased in popularity the dolls were imported in their millions from Germany where the biggest maker seems to have been Armand Marseille. However, Kestner was also a prolific doll maker and a few from his range had yellow boots and these can be expected to fetch a higher price than the more traditional doll with black or brown boots. Most of the Kestner all-bisque dolls have unpainted socks with a blue painted band to signify the tops, though some have blue socks. One pair, believed to date from 1910, with blue painted eyes, two teeth and blond plaited wigs was sold by Christie's in 1987 for £130.

The rarer all-bisque dolls are those that have swivel necks and if they have the French loop moulded into the base of the neck as well then they become that much more sought after and so are valued more highly. The French all-bisque dolls were generally of a higher standard and were mainly peg strung with glass eyes and well painted lashes. They always have good flesh-tinted bisque face and body and exceptional body detailing.

During the colonial period most American dolls were from England, France or Holland having been brought over by early settlers. Sir Richard Grenville presented a European doll to the Roanoke Indians in 1585 and the drawings of John White, who accompanied the expedition, show an Indian girl proudly clutching her Elizabethan doll.

Philadelphia was an early centre of doll production in the first half of the nineteenth century, again using imported German heads but on leather covered bodies made locally. Although the idea of using European parts continued in America it became the home of many technical developments.

The earliest rubber dolls were made by Benjamin

133

A bisque headed googlie eyed doll, 7 inches high marked SK.10. Sold 7 July 1988 for £528. Source: Christie's.

Lee of New York in 1855 and the first celluloid dolls came from John Wesley and Isiah Hyatt a decade later. American manufacturers were also the first to develop rag dolls, stuffed dolls and plastic dolls. Prime examples include:

- the Palmer Cox Brownie from around 1892
- the Kewpie doll (early examples were made mainly of bisque, celluloid and composition and would be worth around £100)
- the Golliwog
- the teddy bear came from the States (see separate heading).

Mechanical dolls with moving limbs and eyes, talking dolls and crying dolls were developed in the States between 1880 and 1910.

More recently costume dolls have come into their own particularly as part of the tourist industry. However the idea of producing clothing, accessories and a wide range of domestic equipment in miniature for dolls' use, dates back more than 100 years. Such items are often valuable as well. Recently a doll's parasol with a bone handle was sold at auction for £250.

Dolls, of course, are more difficult to sell because there are few shops where you can take your find. However, perhaps surprisingly, collecting dolls is widespread and, for instance, in America is second only to stamps in popularity.

Dolls other than French and German – and those produced by Pierrotti and Montanari we mentioned earlier – are collected but not as sought after and so not as valuable. Italian felt dolls by Lenci are quite valuable and you could expect to get around £350 should you find one of these in good condition.

You'll also be looking at something worthwhile if you came across what are called Parisiennes, which were more like models than dolls. They represent adults in miniature, often French ladies which accounts for the name, and good examples of these could be worth as much as £1,000.

The Americans are even interested in collecting quite modern dolls – including those like Cindy from the fifties – but having one of these tucked under the stairs will not result in a major boost to your finances. It is unlikely that an auction house would be interested in such a find but the columns of doll collectors' magazines could well put you in touch with a buyer.

What you are most likely to find in your attic or cupboard is the English version of a bisque doll which would have been produced in Staffordshire around 1910-1930. Unfortunately collectors find these unattractive which will be reflected in the price you'll get. You may well find the only person willing to take it off your hands is a market stall, where the most you can expect is a few pounds.

Surprisingly collectors do not seem attracted by really ancient dolls at the moment which will also affect their current value. However, it is unlikely you will come across dolls from the seventeenth or eighteenth century or even the regency period. These are now very rare and seldom found outside of museums such as the Victoria and Albert in London or the Museum of Childhood in Edinburgh.

One of the quirks of dolls is that they seldom include anything to indicate their sex though, like the majority of customers, they are regarded as being female. However, when dolls are 'sexed' it is the boys that are more sought after than the females.

As with so many of the finds you might make in old houses, discovering the original boxes along with the doll can add to the value of the toy and, in this case, if there are also fine clothes as well then you can expect the price to be quite a big higher than for the doll alone. For example, a normal little Simon and

Halbig girl, with a coronet embroidered on the pinafore (the original owner was given the doll by the Earl of Dudley) along with its original Hamleys' box, fetched £340 in January 1986, around double the anticipated price. Similarly, a 33 inch tall doll in elaborate silk smocked frock and in an original box marked Genuine Walkure Doll went for £950 during the same auction at Christie's – almost double its estimated value.

Teddy Bears

Hidden away in the attics and back-cupboards of homes throughout the country are favourite old teddy bears. They may be moth-eaten, have lost an eye or have some of the stuffing hanging out but woe betide the person who throws them away.

When other toys have long since been cast aside the teddy bear lingers on like the last tenuous link with youth. If the battered and bedraggled creature finds its way to the auction room there will be greetings all round with catalogues describing the poor thing as 'much loved' and customers clamouring to pay exhorbitant prices for something that hardly looked pretty when it was new seventy or so years ago, let alone now.

Teddy bears are, in fact, a fairly recent addition to the playroom. Experts reckon the first one was made in November 1902 and named after Theodore Roosevelt, 26th President of the United States. During his childhood Roosevelt was handicapped by asthma and to compensate he developed a love for big-game hunting. During a 1902 trip to the American south where he was to arbitrate in a border dispute, the President took time off to go bear hunting. All was well until the party came across a tiny bear cub which Roosevelt claimed was too small to shoot.

137

Several members of the press had accompanied the party, among them Clifford K. Berryman, a cartoonist with the *Washington Post*. He drew a cartoon for his paper capturing the event under the caption 'Drawing the Line in Mississippi'. Russian immigrant Morris Michtom, who with his wife ran a small confectionery, novelty and stationery shop in Brooklyn, New York, thought the occasion too good to pass by without something to mark it. His wife made a replica of the cartoon bear with movable arms and legs and a plush covering. The couple put it in their shop window and within five minutes had not only sold the original but received orders for dozens more.

Michtom is reputed to have written to the President asking for permission to market the bears under the name Teddy's Bear. The story goes that Roosevelt, showing an uncharacteristic lack of understanding of his popular appeal wrote back: 'I don't think my name is likely to be worth much in the toy business, but you are welcome to use it.'

Use it Michtom certainly did. One of the largest toy wholesalers in America, Butler Brothers, took on the distribution and gave Michtom credit backing. Within a year sales of the bears had soared and the foundation had been laid for Michtom to build up the Ideal Novelty and Toy Company, which grew into one of the biggest toy manufacturers in America.

However, Michtom is not the only one credited with inventing the teddy bear. Margarete Steiff who was born in Germany in 1847 and was a polio victim as a child, developed her own business so she could remain independent. At first she produced an elephant pincushion but then went on to make other stuffed animals. One of her nephews, Richard, who joined the firm in 1879, enjoyed watching the antics of bear cubs at the zoo and suggested they make a toy bear. Though Margarete had little success with an earlier toy

138

bear she agreed to Richard's new design which included a movable head and limbs.

Another of Margarete's nephews, Paul, was asked to get American reactions to the bears. They were not generally well received, meeting with more criticism than praise. Some of the comments led to alterations before the bears went on show at the Leipzig Toy Fair in 1903. There, one of the biggest New York toy importers George Borgfeldt, placed an order for 3,000 Steiff bears. This time the reactions were better. By the end of 1903 some 12,000 Steiff bears had been sold and so fast did sales grow that in 1907 Steiff bear production reached 974,000.

The German Steiff family's trademark was a yellow metal tag in the bear's ear. Usually this was taken out when the toy was being played with but if still in place it adds greatly to the bear's value. A couple of years ago one complete with its tag was sold in London for £5,280. When it was new in 1904 it had cost the equivalent of just 94p.

Although Roosevelt is generally credited with having been responsible for giving teddy bears their name, there is one suggestion that it might have first been christened in Britain. The story goes that Edward VII saw an Australian koala bear at the zoo, took a liking to it and so it was nicknamed Teddy Bear. Unlikely, but just possible!

In fact the earliest mention of teddy bears in Britain was an advertisement for Morrell's of London's Oxford Street. They advertised 'Old mistress Teddy that lived in a shoe' for Christmas 1909. Then it sold for one guinea (£1.05). Today in good condition it could be worth around £100.

Early teddy bears were long limbed and sturdy so they would easily outlive a single childhood. German bears tend to have long noses while the English ones are more rounded. Usually the fur was soft mohair

A strawberry blonde, plush covered, teddy bear, 12 inches high, with Steiff button in ear, circa 1903/4. Sold 7 July 1988 for £528.
Source: Christie's.

plush – some of the best came from Yorkshire – in gold, cinnamon, black, brown or red with pads of leather, leather cloth or felt. Kapok, woodwool, cork granules, straw and sawdust were used for stuffing. The face had nose and mouth embroidered in black, and glass button eyes.

The German Steiff bears tend to have straighter, longer limbs, felt pads, boot-button eyes and humps. British teddies are usually plumper and more cuddly with more shapely limbs, and some early examples can also have humped backs. The more recent versions have flatter faces and shorter arms.

Well known British manufacturers include:

- William J. Terry, who claimed to be the largest
- J. K. Farnell, one of the earliest in the field with a factory in west London
- Ralph Dunn and Chad Valley who produced six different qualities of teddy bear in 13 sizes during the 1920s.

How much a bear is worth depends, as in the case of most things you'll find in the attic, on its age, condition and desirability. It will be worth extra if it has mechanical features or a growler that still works. The first noise makers were introduced in 1908 and growled when the bear was tipped up. More recently cheaper, press operated squeakers have been introduced.

Collectors are particularly interested in mechanical bears like the acrobatic tumbling bear introduced by Descamps of Paris in 1910. An early example of one of these in reasonable condition could be worth as much as £500. Musical bears of the 1930s, which were generally well made, also attract attention. One in pink plush and a nightcap, with a great deal of character, was sold at Christie's a couple of years ago for £110. It still played a tune when pressed with the thumbs.

Judging the age of a bear gives a clue to its value.

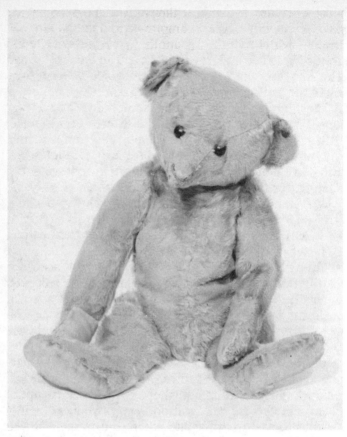

Theodore, a teddy bear in golden plush with boot-button eyes, hump and elongated limbs, 13 inches high with Steiff button in ear, circa 1907. Sold 22 September 1988 for £528. Theodore was arrested in Paris in 1940 as a British subject and spent four years in a prison camp; after a terrifying 14-day train journey to Lisbon in 1944 during which they were straffed by the R.A.F. he was repatriated to Liverpool on a Swedish Red Cross Ship.
Source: Christie's.

One way is by looking at the fur. Although there are exceptions, most early examples were made of mohair. The length of the arms is another clue, with really old teddy bears having paws that reach to midway down the legs with the lower half of the arm curving away from the body. Early bears also had very large feet set at right angles to the legs and original examples will have shaped legs tapering to slim ankles which began to disappear in the 1930s.

One of the worst areas on a bear for wear is the felt pads on the paws. Too much wear here, or holes in the fur, can lead to a loss of shape so it may not be possible to see if the bear was originally hump-backed, a sign of it being an early example. However, if you gently lift the fur on the top of the bear's back you should be able to feel the spare material.

Most pre-1915 teddy bears seem to have had black button eyes but don't despair if your example has glass eyes. They may have been replacements and you can confirm this by feeling around the sockets. Only if the eye is firmly embedded can you be sure that it is the original, and even then there can be some doubt.

Even a patched, holed or bald teddy bear can be worth money. However, do not try to repair it yourself as you may damage it further and reduce its value. There are experts who will do this for you but selling the bear in its original state may be just as rewarding as having the work done first.

Run-of-the-mill bears made in the past forty years are of little value, though you may still get £15 or £20 if it's an interesting example. What you really need to find to be on the track of a money-spinner is either an older bear, one from a famous maker like Steiff, or an unusual one like the 3.5 inch one sold at Christie's at the end of 1985. Its head came off to reveal a lipstick and it had a powder compact in the tummy. That fetched £280.

Some companies have made limited editions of replica bears produced by famous makers. In 1980 Steiff issued 11,000 reproductions of its first teddy bear called 'Papa Bear'. They sold for £35 each. Today, if still in its original box with its numbered certificate and distinctive ear tag, one would fetch well over £300. Another Seiff limited edition, a silver-grey bear that cost £32 in 1985 would be worth more than double that if still in mint condition.

If the bear you find still has a label or a tag then that will easily help you identify it and should give some indication of its value. If you are in any doubt it is best to get the advice of experts. There are specialist museums and the teddy bear repairers will help. So, too, will auction houses like Christie's. If the bear is not worth auctioning they will give you a rough guide to its price and tell you to take it to a local market stall.

However, according to the experts at Christie's it's amazing what a teddy bear 'find' will do for people. Suddenly they decide to become collectors and far from throwing out their old toys they start hunting out 'friends' who can be added to the bear family.

CHAPTER ELEVEN:
END PIECES

Clearly there's no way that we could cram into this single publication all the bits and pieces that you might find lurking in the corners of your home. If you have enjoyed what you've read so far then let the publisher know and maybe we can produce a second volume covering many more subjects. Meanwhile here are a few pointers on a couple of topics which we haven't been able to cover in great detail this time round but which regularly feature in letters and enquiries to both the Mirror and Christie's.

Books

Very few of the books discovered lying around in people's homes turn out to be worth money. First editions are the things that really attract attention and the bids at auction. Unfortunately there were many very fine books printed in the Victorian era which were beautifully illustrated but which are just not sought after by collectors. Those that cover specialist subjects may attract attention but it would be very difficult to give any guidance as to prices.

Don't assume just because a book looks old and particularly well produced that it will fetch money. However, if you are in any doubt then the professionals at Christie's South Kensington, London branch are happy to give the benefit of their knowledge.

Postcard: West Pier, Brighton.

Carpets and Rugs

In general, these are not worth anything. However, they are frequently included in sales at Christie's South Kensington though they do usually need to be a little special to make it. Preferably Turkish, Persian, Russian or Chinese though I'm sure I spotted some old Belgian rugs and carpets when I was last at one of these sales. Again the experts will give you guidance and they do tour the country holding open days at other Christie's branches.

Furniture

This book is about the sort of things that you might find tucked away in the attic so you have good reason to question the inclusion of a section on furniture. After all you are unlikely to find a sideboard or a table and chairs hidden away. Or are you? True enough the average household knows just what furniture it has. However, evidence from the auction houses – and those who travel around the country with the Antiques Roadshow – indicates that people do have items of furniture which they have inherited or bought at secondhand shops. Initially they like the look of them but eventually they are curious about any possible value.

Interest in antique furniture by the general public has only really been in evidence for about twenty years but there is no holding it back now that it has surfaced. That's clearly shown by the increasing number of auctions that take place both in London and around the country. People are keen to know the value of their possessions to they can insure them and many also want to cash in on other's interest. One of the driving forces has been the way furniture is now made and the sort of materials used. The arrival on the scene of chipboard and newer materials have left most of

*An early Victorian mahogany secretaire bookcase,
50 inches. Sold 10 August 1988 for £2,860.
Source: Christie's.*

today's offerings with a limited life expectancy. Not so the solid wood pieces from the eighteenth, nineteenth and even early twentieth century.

During the past couple of years the value of antique furniture has steadily increased following spectacular rises in the early 1980s. The value of the pound plays an important part in this market for interest in old British furniture from overseas, especially America, is high. Nor does furniture have to be truly antique to attract attention. Good quality reproductions are also in demand and can fetch good sums at auction. A mahogany partner's pedestal desk loosley based on a Hepplewhite design and dating from the early part of this century went for £6,500 when offered at auction in 1985.

Victorian craftsmen were just as keen as those of more recent years to capture the style of years gone by. The nineteenth century gothic revival, for instance, is counted as a style in itself and can command good prices. One set of fourteen George IV mahogany dining chairs in this style were sold for £4,200 in 1986. They were part of a large consignment that went to Christie's from a house in North Wales where most of it had been kept since the day it had been made. Also included was a pair of early Victorian mahogany bedside cabinets also in the Gothic Revival style. These went for £900. Knowing the history of a piece of furniture helps if it comes to auction. However another factor was at work with the bedside cabinets. As houses generally get smaller so people's interest in large items is tending to wane. Therefore smaller items are increasing in value much faster than big ones.

By the end of the nineteenth century dozens of businesses both large and small had sprung up making furniture in a host of differing styles from previous centuries. One of the most noteable was W Charles Tozer of London whose craftsmen used seasoned

A large mahogany breakfront library bookcase, 102 inches. Sold 3 August 1988 for £3,300. Source: Christie's.

materials, but the latest machinery, to copy period items. Tozer concentrated on the styles of the early eighteenth century. Another firm, Edwards and Roberts, concentrated more on the middle 1700s as in the case of two chairs which were auctioned at the end of 1986. They came from a set of eight Chippendale style mahogany chairs and sold for £6,600. Two from a set of twelve Hepplewhite style mahogany dining chairs brought £4,620 when sold at Christie's in 1987. Even abroad furniture makers of the nineteenth century copied earlier styles and the idea has never died. Today some top quality examples are made and can be quite sought after. A couple of years ago a modern olivewood pedestal kneehole desk of Georgian design sold for £2,860 at Christie's.

Furniture is quite often altered during its lifetime, at least older furniture frequently shows that this is true. One of the factors affecting price is therefore the closeness of the item to its original form. Damage may have been repaired and that will reduce the eventual worth. Sometimes early veneers are used on a more recent carcass or vise versa. You may still get a good price but not as much as if it had been in its original form. That is worth remembering with any piece you may have. Don't set about trying to repair it yourself or even having restoration work carried out for you. A mid-Georgian mahogany chest went under the hammer at Christie's in 1987. It was in a terrible condition and required considerable restoration. However it sold for £3,000 compared with similar items that had already been 'tampered with' which sold at the same time for between a sixth and a fifth of the price.

Upholstered furniture will seldom be in good condition unless it has already been restored and recovered. One sign of its quality may be original brass castors by firms like Cope and Collinson. Probably the top makers of Victorian upholstered furniture were Howard and Sons who usually put a label on the underneath of their pieces. You might also find an impressed mark, usually on the inside of one of the back legs or as a stamp on one, if not all, of the castors. A good Victorian sofa may fetch up to £1,000 but the quality, design and condition will play a vital part. Many are more decorative than practical – especially Regency style – being particularly uncomfortable to sit in. We can only guess but it would seem some of our forefathers were keen to put off unwelcome visitors. Even unusual items of Victorian furniture can fetch quite good prices as with an early Victorian walnut stool with petit-point upholstered seat. In 1986 it was sold at auction for £1,400. As the price of Victorian furniture climbs so collectors turn their attention to more recent offerings which accounts for the rising popularity of Art Nouveau and Art Deco furniture. Much of it is of huge proportions and so out of place in today's homes – though perhaps less so in country areas so it may pay to auction such a piece in an out of town sale.

Although books can give an indication of furniture values they can only skim the surface and there are many factors that could affect the value of a specific item. A starting point, however, is to take a photograph of any item you think might be of value particularly of any label or markings, and send it to an auction house like Christie's. Lugging around heavy items is a feat not even to be contemplated and it may be worthwhile getting a reliable local dealer or auctioneer to value your furniture. However, as with most items always get more than one quote and never let yourself be talked into a fast sale.

Do's and Dont's

- Don't alter furniture you have in any way. Repairs and restoration may not add to the value and bad restoration can even detract from it.
- Do seek as many quotes as possible if you plan to sell.

Contacts

A number of publications cover furniture but it is difficult to judge for yourself. The Antiques Trade Gazette, available at selected bookstalls, includes information on forthcoming sales of furniture and other antiques.

Jewellery

This is something that people do come across all the time. Unfortunately the subject is so vast that there is no way to give specific guidance. During the time I have been compiling this book experts have shown me a wide range of jewellery finds. In nearly every case where I have thought they were valueless they have turned out to be genuine treasures and vice versa. One way to judge is to look at the container – the more elaborate it is the more likely the contents are to be treasures. It would also be unusual to find really expensive jewellery thrown casually in a box.

Many gold, silver and enamel items can look like nothing more than costume jewellery if they have been left to gather dust. In the same way gems lose their brilliance particularly if they have been left to rub against each other in a box. This is another field where expert guidance is imperative. Many jewellers will charge for their valuation services but you will be able to get a guide from auction houses where no fee has to be paid. They will also be able to suggest where best to go if you want to sell since very few pieces of jewellery are going to be worth auctioning.

Costume jewellery from the thirties and forties is becoming more popular so while it may not fetch much just yet holding on for a few years could prove worthwhile. Gold has only been hallmarked since the turn of the century so it's quite possible to find genuine gold items from the nineteenth century without any mark on them. A small gold mesh bracelet from the early 1800s was recently sold at auction for £400. Seed pearl was a great favourite in Edwardian times and a pendant might well be worth £60 to £80 while even a little brooch could bring you £40. Around the same time there was a great deal of interest in animal brooches. These were beautifully designed even if only paste was used instead of real diamonds. Prices again can reach £400 for good examples.

Advice from the experts is not to tamper with your finds in an attempt to make them look better. You may damage them or spoil the setting. Here we would suggest you contact Christie's King Street London branch or one of their local offices especially if you unearth a jewel box containing a number of items which the High Street jeweller will almost certainly not be willing to value other than for a reasonable fee.

Musical Instruments

Everything from pianos to violins – especially violins, say the experts – form the huge numbers of enquiries to Christie's during their roadshows. As a subject it is too broad for any guidance to be given in a few words. Once again the only recommendation that makes sense would be to take them along to an auction house or send photographs with detailed descriptions of any design marks, together with a stamped addressed envelope, to an auction house.

Paper Money

If you were offered a five shilling note would you be interested? The answer should be a resounding: "Yes". The Treasury printed eight million during the First World War, never issued them and then destroyed most of the notes. However, a few escaped destruction so should you come across one it's anybody's guess how high the bidding would go at auction – but it certainly would go high.

Britain's first £1 and ten shilling notes were issued by the Treasury during the First World War but most people regard 1928 as the start date for our modern paper money since that is the date when the Bank of England took on responsibility for the issue and redemption of all our notes. To mark this new beginning sets of 10s and £1 notes with matching serial numbers were issued. Only a hundred of these pairs are reckoned to have been issued and so they are highly sought after by collectors. One pair in perfect condition was recently sold for £2,000. The very last design Bank of England £1 notes was introduced in 1978. Since it has now been withdrawn from circulation it has become of greater interest to collectors and if you have one with the Prefix DY21 and it's in perfect condition – not circulated at all – then it might be worth as much as £20.

As with so many items of this kind condition is of paramound importance and the value will vary widely between an old dirty crumpled note and a very fine example that has not been in general circulation. A number of books giving values can be found at local libraries and firms like Seaby's, 8 Cavendish Square, London W1M 0AJ, Stanley Gibbons (for address see: Stamps), and the auction houses have experts who can guide you. In addition most of the regular coin magazines include sections on paper money. If your

Postcard: The 4.20 p.m. Rugby Express Passing Harrow.

find includes foreign banknotes then you need to be very careful. Inflation has wrought havoc on a number of occasions as with old German notes and so they are literally not worth the paper they are printed on.

Pictures

What a subject! Even the experts are unable to agree and bidders seem to lose all sense of proportion at times as the price at auction goes soaring sky high. There are stories, of course, of people who have unearthed long lost paintings by famous artists but according to the Christie's people who handle the regular road shows what most people unearth are mere reproductions. They may be very expertly produced but are seldom worth money. By all means have a find checked out but please don't raise any hopes just because it looks old.